THE HONORABLE HEIR

THE HONORABLE HEIR

LAURIE ALICE EAKES

Waterfall
PRESS

Text copyright © 2016 by Laurie Alice Eakes
All rights reserved.

Published by Waterfall Press

www.brilliancepublishing.com

Amazon, the Amazon logo, and Waterfall Press are trademarks of Amazon.com, Inc., or its affiliates.

ISBN-13: 9781503937659
ISBN-10: 1503937658

Cover design by Mike Heath | Magnus Creative

Printed in the United States of America

To Lisa Karen Richardson, writer extraordinaire, for introducing me to Tuxedo Park

AUTHOR'S NOTE

The quotations used at the beginnings of the chapters are taken from the original version of *Etiquette* by Emily Price Post, whose father, the architect Bruce Price, designed many buildings at Tuxedo Park. Mrs. Post spent much of her life in this exclusive fenced community and applied the manners she learned among the wealthiest families of New York society to the principles she recommends in this book of etiquette, which is still the standard for proper behavior nearly a hundred years later. The book is available in the public domain and widely available online. It's written with humor and taste and well worth a read for those interested in a gracious and elegant lifestyle.

CHAPTER 1

Tuxedo Park, New York
November 1, 1900

"The young widow should wear deep crepe for a year and then lighter mourning for six months and second mourning for six months longer. There is nothing more utterly captivating than a sweet young face under a widow's veil, and it is not to be wondered at that her own loneliness and need of sympathy, combined with all that is appealing to sympathy in a man, results in the healing of her heart. She should, however, never remain in mourning for her first husband after she has decided she can be consoled by a second."
Emily Price Post

She felt his gaze upon her from the instant she stepped into the club-house ballroom. That ballroom, all white pillars and blue velvet benches around the circular walls, fell silent the moment Catherine VanDorn, now Lady Bisterne, strolled through the white painted doors from the great hall, and a hundred pairs of eyes swiveled in her direction. Yet the intensity of one man's bold stare drew her own past the gowns and jewels of the New York elite to meet the audacious dark eyes of a gentleman at the far side of the room.

Her heart skipped a beat. Her gold-shod feet stumbled. Skin-deep cold from the rainy November evening crept through to her bones, and for the first time that evening, she accepted that Mama was correct to tell her not to wear the mauve satin ball gown a mere thirteen months after her husband's death. It was too bright, too frivolous, proclaiming, however falsely, that the debutante who had departed from Tuxedo Park in triumph on the arm of an English lord, a scandal in her wake, intended to seek a new husband.

Behind her, her sister Estelle poked Catherine in the spine. "If I have to be here, at least let me in." She spoke in a whisper loud enough for the staring gentleman to hear.

It unleashed a buzz of other voices. A rising tide of exclamations, speculations, and a handful of greetings broke through the waterfall of words. "She doesn't look to be mourning anyone," came from a pretty matron in lavender tulle, and "I wonder whose fiancé she'll run off with this time," emerged from the pouting lips of a slip of a girl in white lace. But Mama's circle of intimate friends glided forward to embrace Catherine in wide sleeves and perfume and niceties like "I know your family is happy to have you here" and "You're too young to stay in blacks forever."

Pompadours and powdered cheeks blocked Catherine's view of the staring gentleman. Warmth began to steal back into her limbs, clear through to her heart, giving her hope that perhaps she could make this homecoming work out well for everyone, especially her family.

She smiled back at the ladies, then some older gentlemen, friends of her parents. She shook hands. Orchestra music rose from the stage, rising into an invitation for the annual ball to commence. Onlookers and interlocutors began to drift away in pairs to take their places in the center of the circular room. Catherine's parents strode off arm-in-arm, a young man claimed his dance with Estelle, and their brother, Paul

Henry VanDorn the Third, claimed the hand of the doll-sized girl in white lace.

Catherine stepped back so her ruffled skirt brushed the blue velvet of a curving bench. She should seat herself and remain unobtrusive after her explosive entrée back into Tuxedo Park society. But sitting felt like surrender. Standing, on the other hand, looked too much as though she were inviting one of the still unattached gentlemen to ask her to dance. Indeed, two youthful-looking males headed in her direction. She glanced away so she didn't meet their eyes, as she had those of the man who had stared without subterfuge, and nearly choked on a suppressed groan that tried to leave her throat.

"You aren't dancing, are you, Lady Bisterne." Delivering the words as a statement, not a question, an older lady who'd worn black for longer than Catherine's twenty-four years, stomped forward with the aid of an amber cane and seized Catherine's hand in a crushing grip. "We may all recover from you returning in mauve, and perhaps even those jewels in your hair, but if you dance tonight, you may as well take yourself back to England, as no one worth knowing will receive you."

Catherine granted the lady a curtsy. "I doubt you'll receive me regardless of whether or not I dance, Mrs. Selkirk."

"Depends."

"On what, ma'am?"

"Whether or not you're sorry for what you did to my granddaughter."

"Oh, I'm sorry if I hurt her."

Though she had, in truth, done Georgette a favor in keeping her from marrying Edwin, the Earl of Bisterne.

"Perhaps she'll let me tell her just how sorry I am." Catherine sought out Georgette Selkirk.

She spotted her gliding around the floor to the rhythm of the Strauss waltz—in the arms of the staring stranger. He caught Catherine's eye and inclined his head before the swirl of dancers carried him and Georgette out of her sight again.

"Is that her new beau she's dancing with?" Catherine asked.

"A mere friend of my grandson's, but Georgette seems to have a growing fondness for him." Mrs. Caroline Selkirk rapped her cane on the floor dangerously close to Catherine's toes. "So keep your distance from Lord Tristram."

"Lord Tristram Wolfe?" Invisible hands seemed to have gotten hold of Catherine's stay laces and drawn them tight enough so she could no longer breathe.

Mrs. Selkirk leaned forward to peer into Catherine's face, though she was a full head shorter. "Do you know him?"

"No, I never met him. But his cousin was with my husband when he died."

And if she didn't get away from Mrs. Selkirk's reek of peppermint and the overcrowded ballroom, Catherine was going to expire right there.

"If you will please excuse me, ma'am . . ." Catherine slid her right foot a few inches over in preparation to glide out of Mrs. Selkirk's reach. "I should ensure my sister's instruments have gotten stowed away behind the stage safely." She added a smile to convince the older lady of the truth of her words. "Would you like to sit for the upcoming performance?"

The cane thumped on the floor loudly enough that it could have been the bass drum in the orchestra. "I'd like you to assure me you won't hurt my granddaughter again."

"On the contrary, I wish to make amends for the past." Catherine steeled herself against rejection. "May I call on your family in the near future?"

"I don't want you near our house." The clipped words and thump of the cane resounded like blows against Catherine's heart.

She winced, blinking hard against blurriness in her eyes, and half turned away. "Then I'll be on my way." Neither waiting for a fare-thee-well nor permission to depart the older lady's company, she swept around fast enough to send the green-velvet-trimmed ruffles on the bottom half of her skirt flaring out like a dozen fans.

With Estelle swooping around the ballroom floor, Catherine did need to ensure her younger sister's instruments had reached the clubhouse. Being allowed to provide part of the night's entertainment, along with some of the other young people from Tuxedo Park, was the only real reason why Estelle agreed to attend the ball that launched her into society. If so much as a fingerprint marred the cello, violin, or the banjo especially, Estelle would leave the launching of the season, even if she had to walk uphill to her home at Lake House through the rain. Having endured enough trouble getting Estelle to the festivities, Catherine was not about to let her younger sister conduct herself with even a hint of scandalous behavior.

Catherine slipped around a group of gawking young men she didn't recognize and headed for the doorway.

"Heed my warning." Old Mrs. Selkirk's voice rang out in the sudden lull as the waltz concluded.

She heeded. She heeded. She heeded. She would have to find a way other than a social call in order to talk to her old friend. Right now, she needed to escape from Mrs. Selkirk and the folly of her imprudent decision to wear mauve and green to announce she had left first mourning a few months early. Around her, the crowd eddied and flowed like wavelets on the shore. Several people nodded greetings to her. She returned the salutations and continued to flit past and around the handful of guests between her and the exit.

"Lady Bisterne." A drawling English voice cut through the hubbub of the throng. An all-too-familiar voice.

Her heart lurched in her chest like a badly sprung carriage. She halted and turned back toward the speaker, for not doing so would be insufferably rude. He strode toward her with two other gentlemen in tow. Before them, the company parted as though the men were royalty.

They weren't. Two of them could scarcely call themselves part of the aristocracy. She didn't know the third gentleman. Even if his looks likely opened any door he wanted, his choice of friends didn't recommend him as someone she wanted to meet, nor did the fact he'd stared at her upon her arrival.

"What are you doing here, Ambrose?" In as chilly a voice as she could muster, she addressed the man who had called to her, the man who had been with her husband when he died.

He stopped before her and bowed. "I had an invitation to visit this fair land so took advantage of it."

"How nice for you." Her tone was sweet. Her stomach churned. "And you didn't come alone."

Ambrose's teeth flashed in a grin. "You know I never liked being alone."

Neither did she, but she had been for too many years, thanks to men like Ambrose Wolfe.

"I have my cousin with me." He gestured to the stranger in the mix. "Lord Tristram Wolfe."

She'd never met the younger son of the Marquess of Cothbridge, but she'd heard of him, mostly in less than favorable terms. He was rather better looking than the gossip rags led her to believe. He was rather better than good-looking, with high cheekbones, a square jaw, and eyes the color of fine, dark Chinese jade in perfect contrast to hair the color of caramel sauce with a rather delightful cowlick.

"Pleased to finally meet you, my lady." Lord Tristram bowed.

"How do you do?" She dropped a perfunctory curtsy, then glanced at the third man, her husband's cousin, Florian Baston-Ward.

He sidled closer to take her gloved hand and raise it to his lips. "Cousin Kate, I see you've come out of mourning already, complete with wearing stolen Bisterne jewels."

Later, Lord Tristram would take Florian to task for tipping his hand about the jewels. For now, he saved his concentration for the lady and how she responded to the careless remark.

"Stolen?" Other than that single word and a widening of her long-lashed eyes, Lady Bisterne gave no telling reaction. Her complexion maintained its porcelain purity. No color drained from her cherry-ice-colored lips, and her gaze remained fixed on Florian's face. In short, she didn't look guilty despite the fact that two of the jeweled pieces Tristram had crossed half of Europe and then the Atlantic to find shimmered and sparkled against her rather glorious dark auburn hair.

"Not a discussion for the ballroom." Tristram tore his regard from the lady to scowl at the younger son of his mother's cousin and his father's oldest friend. "Badly done of you, Baston-Ward. You should ask her to dance, not make careless accusations."

"I'm not dancing," she said at the same time Florian exclaimed, "You expect me to ask her to dance? It's bad enough she's wearing colors—"

"Florian, be nice." Ambrose punched the younger man in the shoulder.

"Go foist yourself on some pretty American girl." Tristram added his voice to Ambrose to be rid of the youth and leave him alone with Lady Bisterne.

Florian's blue eyes flashed with lightning. "When she left me penniless?" He waved a hand toward her ladyship. "No American girl would be interested in me."

"Try a wallflower." Tristram glanced around to locate the inevitable row of young ladies with whom no one wished to dance because of their poor looks or their lack of money.

A lack of money wasn't prevalent in that land of the elite wealthy. Some plain-faced young women did perch on the edges of the cushions as though about to jump up and run, or lounged back as though they wanted to sit out the dance. One of the latter wasn't plain faced at all.

Indeed, she looked too much like Catherine, Lady Bisterne, not to be related.

"I see any number of young ladies not dancing." Tristram jostled Florian's elbow to get him thinking with reason about going away.

Florian opened his mouth as though to protest, then shut it again and stalked off toward the wallflower row. Ambrose followed with a mumbled, "Wouldn't mind another dance or two myself."

Tristram turned back, but Lady Bisterne had gone. She'd been heading for the door when Ambrose had waylaid her, presuming upon their acquaintance back in England. Tristram could follow her. He should follow her in the event she disposed of those bejeweled combs in her hair. Not that doing so would change the fact that she wore them, that a hundred people had seen her wearing them like she possessed a right to do so.

Tristram's mouth hardened, and he headed for the exit. The sooner he learned the truth from her ladyship, the sooner he could return home and settle matters with his father.

"You're not going to go hide away with the old men, are you, Tris?" His host, Pierce Selkirk, clapped Tristram on the shoulder. "Never used to be the type to drink spirits and smoke cigars."

Tristram shuddered. "Not in the least." A fact that hadn't gone over well with his fellow army officers. "I wished to . . ." He trailed off, unwilling to admit he wished to go after a lady. Ambrose and Florian knew why he was there in Tuxedo Park, but to his host, Pierce, his friend from university, he was doing what hundreds of other titled men from all over Europe had been doing in the past decade or two—looking for an American heiress as a wife.

Not that he would object to one if he loved her. If he found the proof he needed that Lady Bisterne had stolen the jewels from her late husband's family. If he met his father's requirements to prove his younger son could succeed at something, even if Tristram had failed to bring military glory to the family.

Pierce was watching him with one sandy brow raised in enquiry, and Tristram struggled for a truthful response. "I wish to avoid another dance so soon." He touched the back of his head, where his hair now sprang up in an unruly cowlick from a ridge of scarring beneath.

"Ah, the old head not up to more twirling about?" Pierce laughed. "Mine doesn't like it much either, and I don't even have your excuse. But no worries. After this dance, there'll be an entertainment. Some of the younger set will perform."

"Sounds like a good reason to escape."

"Most of it, yes, but Miss VanDorn is worth listening to." Pierce's gaze flicked to the dance floor and an auburn-haired young lady whirling about with Florian.

Lady Bisterne's sister.

"She's an extraordinary talent," Pierce added.

"And pretty. Do I detect some interest there?" Tristram smiled.

"About as much as you have in my sister."

Tristram's smile died. Fortunately, the music faded to a close. Dancers and chaperones cleared from the dance floor and politely jockeyed for seats on the blue velvet benches along the walls. Abandoning their partners to their own families, Georgette, Ambrose, and Florian joined Tristram and Pierce near the doorway.

"Miss VanDorn is one of the performers." Florian's eyes gleamed. "She plays the banjo. I've never heard one."

"They're all the rage with the ladies here." Pierce grimaced. "Most should burn theirs."

"Burn instruments?" Both Florian and Ambrose protested such a notion, being musicians themselves.

"Pierce is referring to my attempts." Georgette's sweet voice held a laugh. "But Estelle is quite different. You'll enjoy her part. Now, do excuse me. I see Grandmother beckoning to me."

The old lady waved her cane in their direction, much to the peril of those around her.

"She's going to brain someone with that one day. Sometimes I think—"

Lights in the ballroom darkened except for over the stage. A hush settled throughout the attendees, and several young ladies in fluttery white dresses filed onto the stage escorted by young men with dark coats and stiff collars. From behind them, an unseen musician gave them a pitch, and the chorus began to sing in voices angelic enough to grace any church.

A theatrical sketch followed the ballads. When she forgot her lines, the leading lady dissolved into nervous titters. As though this were part of the drama, the audience laughed with—or perhaps at—her, someone prompted her from the rear of the stage, and she proceeded without another hitch.

"How long does this go on?" Ambrose whispered a little too loudly.

Tristram elbowed him in the ribs. "You'll never catch an American wife if you are rude."

"I'll never catch an American wife without a title," Ambrose countered. "Even your poor excuse of a courtesy title is worth something here."

"I think—" Florian began.

Several people nearby hushed him.

The attention of the guests shifted from polite to interested, with those standing slipping a step or two closer to the stage and some of those previously seated standing, as pretty Miss VanDorn glided onto the stage.

She settled a peculiar-looking stringed instrument onto her lap and began to play. She played it like a professional musician. The notes hummed and trilled and tumbled over one another like gemstones caught in a waterfall. At the conclusion of each piece, the audience applauded with the enthusiasm the performance deserved. After three selections, Miss VanDorn rose, bowed, then swept off stage.

Lights from the chandeliers overhead blazed through the room. Like wind from an approaching storm, voices rose to fill the circular chamber. On the stage, the orchestra returned, while on the dance floor, the guests began to mill about and again pair off.

Ambrose punched Tristram's arm. "Time to start solving your mystery, Sherlock Holmes."

Tristram shook his head. "There is no mystery here. I need to gather my proof, or we can take no action against an American dowager countess." He scanned the room for that countess. Surely she had returned to hear her sister's performance. If she had, though, she must have entered from somewhere near the stage, or she would have passed by his position near the doors. With his height advantage, he should have been able to see her. But no jeweled combs flashed in dark reddish-brown hair. Pierce had wandered off, so Tristram was free to leave the ballroom in search of Catherine, Lady Bisterne.

"Oh no you don't, Lord Tristram." Georgette swooped up beside him, her sky-blue eyes sparkling. "We need all the men we can catch to stay and continue partnering the debutantes. Let me introduce you to a few."

Those debutantes seemed to consist of a few dozen ladies of all ages. Whether cool matron or giggling girl, one factor they shared was their reaction to learning he could, by way of his father's status, place "Lord" in front of his first name. Their smiles widened, their fans fluttered faster, and they leaned a little closer.

Weary of Georgette Selkirk shepherding him forward like a lost lamb, Tristram chose a plain but lively young lady to be his partner in the first set. Miss Hudock executed the figures of the dance with light steps and not a great deal of chatter.

"You've likely already seen what Tuxedo Park has to offer, my lord, so do tell me about where you live. Is it a castle?"

Tristram laughed. "It's rather a larger and older version of many of the houses I see here in the Park. Half-timber."

"And stone. Yes, isn't it pretty? How old?"

"Three hundred and twenty years." He talked as they rounded the circular ballroom.

How many dancers grew dizzy or lost their way without sides and corners?

"It belongs to my father, though, not me." He scanned the room for Lady Bisterne or her sister, still not seeing them.

"The windows are rather gray because the glass is so old."

"Will it be yours one day?"

"Not if God and I see eye to eye on the issue." They passed the entrance door, one of the few landmarks to give him spatial perspective on the room.

Before him, the young lady's gray eyes widened. "You don't want to own a manor house?"

Only for the good he could do with the income. But he didn't think she would understand that.

"Sometimes," he admitted. "A great deal of responsibility and privilege comes with it."

"My papa says privilege is a form of responsibility." She spoke as the music slowed and ended.

"You have a wise papa." Tristram bowed, and when he straightened, he caught a glimpse of pinkish-purple satin through a door near the stage.

With more haste than the charming lady deserved, he returned her to her mama, then skirted the room as quickly as he could manage without knocking anyone over. Still, when he reached the doorway, he didn't see a sign of her ladyship's luxurious gown.

He did, however, catch a glimpse of something sparkling against the floorboards.

In two strides, he reached the gemstones and scooped them up. Diamonds sparkled and gold and pearls gleamed against his white glove. Above the teeth of the comb, the setting arched on a twist at the edges, an unusual design. Save for its partner comb, a unique setting brought into the Bisterne family over a hundred years earlier. It belonged to the estate, the new Earl of Bisterne, his father's oldest friend. Yet the twenty-four-year-old Dowager Countess of Bisterne calmly walked off with this and a host of other jewels that did not belong to her.

Tristram curled his fingers around the comb until the filigree setting and stones marred his gloves. Eyes narrowed, he scanned the corridor for her larcenous ladyship.

"I'll find you before you can rid yourself of the other comb." He headed down the great hall, nearly empty during the dance. Despite Georgette's claims, this early in the evening, most of the men hadn't abandoned the ladies in pursuit of more manly diversions.

But her ladyship appeared to have abandoned the festivities. Tristram spotted her on the other side of the massive fireplace and stalking toward the clubhouse's front door.

He started after her. A few older gentlemen and couples impeded his progress and line of sight. He paused, his way blocked by a cluster of young people. "I beg your pardon, but may I please get through?"

"We're terribly sorry." They started back as though he'd spoken a foreign language. A gap formed he could pass through.

Nodding his thank-you, Tristram lengthened his stride. "Lady Bisterne." He kept his voice low.

She either didn't hear him or chose to ignore him.

"My lady?"

She grasped the faceted crystal doorknob.

Tristram closed his free hand over hers, feeling the chill of her fingers through the thin gloves. "I wouldn't do that if I were you."

She emitted a squeak of a gasp and reared back. Her other comb lost its anchor on her hair and dropped to the floor with a clatter.

"What are you doing?" She yanked her hand free and clapped her hands to hair still anchored by pearl-headed pins.

"I need to talk to you about this." He held out the first comb, then stooped to collect the other.

She set her foot upon it. "These were a wedding present from my late husband. That is all you need to know."

"That's not what the new earl claims."

"The new earl may—" An odd crunch crackled loudly enough to be heard over the orchestra and dancers. Her ladyship drew her brows together over a nose falling just short of perfect, took a step back and stared at the floor.

Where an elaborate hair ornament of diamonds and pearls had lain but moments earlier, now lay a twisted gold setting and shards so small they came close to qualifying as dust.

CHAPTER 2

"The groom buys the handsomest ornament he can afford—a string of pearls if he has great wealth, or a diamond pendant, brooch or bracelet, or perhaps only the simplest bangle or charm—but whether it is of great or little worth, it must be something for her personal adornment." Emily Price Post

Catherine's head seemed to detach from her neck and begin to float somewhere over her body, part of it staring at the crushed, obviously artificial gems on the floor, part of her listening to music, voices, laughter, part of her inhaling the spiciness of a chrysanthemum bouquet and the sandalwood warmth of the man before her. Beneath her, the heels of her shoes seemed to have come loose. They wobbled. She swayed.

Warm, strong hands closed over her shoulders. "Are you going to faint, my lady?"

"Yes. No. I've never fainted in my life." She raised her hands to press her palms on either side of her head and hold it firmly in place. "I am not going to faint over a little bit of deception on my husband's behalf. It won't be the first time I caught him in a lie." A bubble of laughter rose in her throat. She gulped it down, and tears filled her eyes. "Excuse me. I need some air." She jerked free of his hands on her shoulders, flung open the door too quickly for him to stop her this time, and propelled herself onto the porch.

The mist had turned to rain. It pattered in cold and steady ribbons beyond the sheltering roof. She shivered, took a deep breath of the bracing air—

And remembered her sister.

"Estelle. Oh no, I need to find Estelle. She didn't return to the ballroom after her performance." She glanced around seeking a white dress by the light of a few lamps burning beneath the ceiling.

"She must be inside." Lord Tristram joined her on the porch. "It's too cold and wet out here for anyone to linger." He touched Catherine's elbow. "Come back inside. I'll help you find her. Could she have rejoined the dancers while you were in the hall?"

"I don't know. She promised me she'd stay. If she's run off into this rain—" She made herself stop babbling and take a deep breath. "One of Estelle's friends said she saw her heading for the door."

Catherine wouldn't doubt for a minute that her younger sister was perfectly capable of convincing the coachman to take her home. She might even take advantage of all of them being occupied at the ball to carry out a threat she had made upon Catherine's arrival home.

I want to run away and be on my own like you did.

She didn't seem to understand that, with Catherine, running away meant a wealthy and titled female traveling across Europe with her lady's maid, an acceptable activity for a new widow. With Estelle, a young lady did not run off on her own to join a group of musicians.

"I expect once she saw the weather," Lord Tristram said, "she would have gone back inside."

"That's what a sensible person would do, but Estelle is not sensible." Catherine turned back toward the door, sensible enough herself to get in out of the rain.

Lord Tristram opened it for her. She swept over the threshold and caught the sparkle of paste gemstone fragments still glittering on the floor, scattered by long skirts and feet. Those fragments were all that remained of the gift that had held so much promise for a nineteen-year-old girl with little sense and lots of vanity. They were another lie, another disappointment, another shattering of a dream.

And Florian Baston-Ward, her late husband's cousin, had accused her of taking the jewels. She must put a stop to such a rumor or her family would suffer. If Estelle ran away, she and the rest of the family would suffer.

If some ancient warrior suddenly appeared in the corridor with a battle ax and sliced her in two, Catherine doubted she could feel more divided than she did at that moment. Stop Florian from his not-so-veiled accusations, or find Estelle?

"Find Estelle," she said aloud.

"I'll help you, my lady."

"Why?"

He shrugged. "Why not?"

"The reasons are numerous. Because you are a stranger. Because you're an English aristocrat. Because you and your friend rather accused me of stealing Bisterne jewels."

"All that aside, a missing young lady is still a missing young lady."

Catherine stared at him, gazed into eyes rimmed in gold-tipped lashes that lent them a sunny warmth. Soft, gentle eyes that did not flinch from her direct stare even after what she had just said.

"All English noblemen and their sons are not created equally, Lady Bisterne." His voice, with its clear, precise speech borne of generations of careful breeding and training, still managed to sound as gentle and warm as his eyes appeared.

She felt a little warm. Her mind settled its frantic rushing from one crisis to another, and her spine felt straightened by more than her corset.

"Thank you." She glanced through the ballroom doorway. The dancers spun by in a graceful kaleidoscope of color, with the orchestra soaring in the background. "I thought she might be with the musicians.

That is, she likes to talk to members of the orchestras and bands at these galas."

"She's a talented young lady."

"She is. But she wasn't in the back rooms where the musicians were before their performances. And I don't see her in the ballroom. She's tall enough that she usually stands out."

"And I'm tall enough that I can usually see what I'm looking for."

He stood a full head taller than she, even though she wore heeled slippers.

"Where else might she have gone?" Lord Tristram glanced at the staircase. "Up there?"

"It's a good place to start." She headed for the steps. Her toe kicked something on the floor. Gold flashed as the filigree setting of the comb sailed across the hall. She grasped the newel post with one hand and swallowed against a burning in her throat, blinked against a burning in her eyes. She could not accept that the gift she had cherished through all those lonely years of her marriage turned out to be a fake. Yet Florian Baston-Ward accused her of taking them.

Lord Tristram stooped and retrieved the bit of mangled gold. "We'll talk about this later."

"I have no idea why I should talk to you about my husband's perfidy." To form her response, she employed all the hauteur she had learned in her four years as the wife of a peer.

With all the hauteur of the peerage he had been raised to potentially inherit as a younger son, he responded, "I think you will."

For a moment, their eyes met, held. His remained calm and warm. She hoped hers told him to kindly remove himself from her presence. Since he remained right where he was, she must have failed.

She couldn't waste more time on him. Pretending he wasn't following her, she headed up the wide, polished treads once used for indoor tobogganing until some young lady had shown too much petticoat lace and a young man commented on it. Ah, the silliness of youth.

The silliness of youth—Estelle's—kept Catherine climbing to the second floor and the range of private rooms for anything from gentlemen withdrawing to smoke their cigars, to young ladies needing a place with maids standing by to repair a torn flounce or pin up a tumbled lock of hair. A remote chance might have led Estelle into this latter room, and Catherine opened the door wide enough to peek around the edge. Only two maids stood in anticipation of someone entering for assistance.

"Has Miss VanDorn been in here?" Catherine asked.

"No, ma'am." The maid bobbed a curtsy. "I haven't seen her tonight."

Catherine thanked her and closed the door to the momentarily empty corridor. Lord Cothbridge's younger son had vanished from sight. Good. Estelle was none of his concern. Catherine's artificial jewels were none of his concern. She could not imagine why he acted as though they were.

She glanced up and down the passage. It remained empty—empty, but not quiet. Music from the ballroom soared from below along with the rise and fall of voices in conversation and laughter. The rumble of male voices and stench of smoke seeped from beneath a door further down the hall. Estelle would never set foot inside there, even if the men allowed her to. Catherine proceeded to the rooms she truly feared Estelle might occupy—ones not officially employed for the evening. If she had sneaked into one to hide and practice her music, not much harm would have been done. But Estelle wasn't above collecting musicians to accompany her, regardless of who the person was and with little regard to propriety. Few of the Tuxedo Park residents played music seriously enough for Estelle, so she took advantage of whom she could.

"But not at the autumn ball." Catherine spoke aloud, and her voice rang out in a lull in the music and conversation below. But from a chamber down the hall, bows drew across a cello and violin, and at the same time Lord Tristram stepped into the corridor and beckoned to Catherine.

Feet dragging as though she were a child about to be punished for some infraction, she closed the distance between them. "Is she in there?"

Even Estelle couldn't play two instruments at once.

"She's here." He raised a hand and flattened his cowlick. It sprang back the instant he removed his hand. "She is, um, not alone." His unflappable demeanor seemed to have deserted him.

A cloud of butterflies swarming in her middle, Catherine said, "And she's not alone."

"No." His tone held an odd note, surprise or maybe annoyance.

Catherine reached for the door.

Lord Tristram opened it for her. "Lady Bisterne." He announced her as though he were a butler and she were arriving at afternoon tea with a duchess.

The cello ceased. Its owner stood, and Catherine flung out one hand to grip the doorframe. "Florian?"

He bowed. "The same, my lady."

And from just beyond Florian, Ambrose Wolfe stood bowed as well, a violin tucked under one arm. Between them, Estelle remained seated, her banjo perched on her lap, her lips curved in a smile of satisfaction. For several moments, they stood like posed manikins, then Catherine broke the tableau.

"What are you doing in here alone with two gentlemen you scarcely know?"

Estelle sighed. "If someone wishes to play music, what does formality matter?"

"Propriety." Catherine resisted the urge to snatch the banjo from her sister and take it someplace where she couldn't retrieve it. "And your word. You promised me you would stay for one set of dances after the performance."

"I did." A dimple appeared in Estelle's right cheek. "I didn't promise I'd dance."

Someone snickered.

"We will discuss this when we are not in front of strangers." Catherine flicked her gaze from her sister to first one gentleman and then the other.

Mr. Wolfe and Florian refused to meet her eyes. Beside her, Lord Tristram stood with hands on his hips and his mouth set in a grim line. "I do believe," he said, "my fellow guests have forgotten their manners."

"Considering how Florian greeted me," Catherine said, "I believe at least he didn't come with his." She took a step toward her cousin by marriage. "Tell me, why did you accuse me of stealing those jeweled combs?"

"I recalled them from the family jewels that belong to the estate." His gaze flicked to her hair. "They, like the rest of the jewels, went missing with Edwin's death . . . And now, what did you do with them?"

"Lord Tristram has one." Catherine steeled herself against the pain of betrayal reawakened. "And I accidentally broke the other one."

"So long as it can be repaired," Florian began.

"No." Catherine shook her head. "It can't be repaired. I stepped on it, and the jewels smashed."

Florian paled. "They were artificial?"

"As useless as library paste," Lord Tristram interjected.

And Mr. Ambrose Wolfe's bow went sailing across the room to crack against the wall.

∞

Music and chatter rose like smoke from the ballroom below. If it weren't for the din of the party, the withdrawing room at the top of the Tuxedo Park clubhouse would have been quiet enough to hear a mouse scuttling through the cellars. Silent, still, and nearly motionless. Only everyone's eyes moved.

From beneath half-lowered lids, Tristram observed his companions regarding one another, while avoiding meeting anyone's eyes. If not for those shifting gazes, they would have resembled a staged tableau or set of schoolboys who had dared one another not to be the first to break the imitation of garden statuary.

As the eldest at twenty-eight, Tristram should break the stalemate. On the other hand, Lady Bisterne held social precedent to do so. She might not realize that, even after four years in England and another on the Continent.

If she did know and chose not to end the impasse of wills, and Tristram took matters into his hands, he would be insufferably rude.

How long the five of them would have sat or stood like salt sculptures Tristram didn't know, for in the corridor, someone shouted unintelligible words and others laughed. Lady Bisterne startled, and her hand slapped the door, slamming it all the way shut. Everyone jumped.

Ambrose laughed. "So how do I go about replacing this bow?"

"In the city." Estelle began to pluck soft notes from the strings of her banjo. "Tuxedo Park is sadly lacking in music."

"Not with you here, Miss—"

"Florian." Tristram snapped out the younger man's name to stop the flattery. "Lady Bisterne and Miss VanDorn do not need you interfering here. You either, Ambrose. We should repair to the ballroom."

"And dance with young ladies who won't look twice at me because I don't have a title." Ambrose's lips turned down at the corners.

"They would if they heard you play the violin." Miss VanDorn gave him a positively worshipful look.

Lady Bisterne touched her gloved fingertips to a loose strand of hair fluttering charmingly over one ear, shook out the skirt of her ruffled gown as though it were coated in dust, then stepped forward, her head high, her round, cleft chin thrust out and her shoulders drawn back.

"Put your instruments away and bid goodnight to these gentlemen." Her clear, deep-blue glance flicked from Florian to Ambrose. "I use the term as a courtesy, as you're considered gentlemen in England. Here, however, you have not behaved like gentlemen in coming to this room alone with a young lady. Do not do anything of the like again."

"Catherine." Miss VanDorn's face flamed. "You have no business in scolding them."

"Actually," Tristram said, "she does, as the social superior in this room."

"This is America. We don't hold with such ceremony." Miss VanDorn began a complicated fingerpicking pattern on her five-stringed instrument. "We believe in equality."

"Which is why half the debutantes in the country want to marry European titles," Ambrose drawled.

Tristram glared at Ambrose. "Enough, cousin." He bowed to her ladyship. "I'll take care of this riffraff"—he indicated the two younger men—"if you wish to see to your sister."

"Thank you." Lady Bisterne smoothed out a wrinkle in her glove, then tapped her fingers against the fragile wrist beneath. "Estelle, put up your banjo and return to the ballroom."

Miss VanDorn continued to play. "You know I detest dancing. All the others besides these two who've ask me to dance tonight have no sense of timing with the music."

"We'll sign your card for the rest of the night," Ambrose and Florian said in unison.

They sounded so absurd, so young and eager, Tristram laughed. "I think that would prove unacceptable."

"Indeed." If anything, Lady Bisterne's chin edged higher. "But they may escort us downstairs and carry the instruments."

Ambrose and Florian jumped to comply.

Tristram's gaze flicked to Lady Bisterne's expressive chin, where a cleft dimpled the roundness. It appeared as though a fingertip had pressed into the mold of her features to keep them from appearing too perfect, to give them character. Tristram's forefinger twitched as though he would trace that flaw and test the porcelain smoothness of her complexion.

He tucked his hands behind his back. "You lads should dance with Miss Selkirk, you know."

"To get her away from you?" Florian grinned.

Lady Bisterne paled. "I forgot you are staying with the Selkirks. You had best go do your duty by Georgette. I will assist Estelle."

"You can't carry a cello downstairs any more than I can." Estelle's glance was scornful. "Mr. Baston-Ward and Mr. Wolfe shall assist me, since it's neither of them Georgette is interested in."

"No titles," the younger two men chorused.

Lady Bisterne's complexion appeared paler than the pearls around her neck, and she stooped to gather up the broken bow, her skirts billowing around her like petals.

"Do help the ladies, you two." Tristram looked at the pieces of the bow and opened his mouth to ask Ambrose why he had broken it, then silenced himself. He could talk to his cousin at any time regarding his poor behavior. Not so Lady Catherine Bisterne. Instead of nonsensical notions of touching that cleft in her ladyship's chin, he must remind himself that she was the reason for his presence in Tuxedo Park, New York. She was his prime suspect, and he needed to talk to her about it in an environment where they would not so easily be distracted or interrupted, not easy in this inhospitable November climate, as any tête-à-tête in a drawing room risked both distraction and interruption. Country walks proved far more convenient for private dialogue, but not in freezing rain. Difficulties with a meeting did not negate that he needed one, especially after the events of this evening.

He might get the opportunity tonight, for with alacrity, Ambrose and Florian began replacing the violin and cello in their cases, and Miss

VanDorn did the same with her banjo. Lady Bisterne stood staring at the broken bow as though not certain what it was or what to do with it. She looked like someone who had no intention of going anywhere.

Tristram took a step toward her, his intention to ask her if they could talk.

She thrust the bow at Ambrose. "Let Estelle and me go before you two, lest our reputations suffer." She strode to the door, beckoning to her sister to follow.

Slowly, Miss VanDorn followed.

Her ladyship was right. He couldn't talk to her alone there. Eagerness to solve this problem with the jewels and get away from Tuxedo Park before Georgette got her hopes raised in his direction were clouding his good sense.

He reached the door before she did and touched her arm. "May I call upon you tomorrow, my lady?"

"Call?" She faced him, patting at her hair where one of the combs had helped pearl-headed pins hold up her masses of glossy waves. "If you intend to explain your ridiculous charges, then yes, you may. Eleven thirty. No one will be around then."

"Thank you." Tristram bowed and opened the door. "Good evening, ladies. If we do not see you in the ballroom, we shall see you tomorrow." He closed the door, then leaned against it, his arms crossed over his chest. He glared at Ambrose and Florian. "What were the two of you thinking? You know better than to be alone with a young lady, especially someplace so public."

"We found a way to get into the good graces of a pretty heiress," Florian said.

"We aren't heirs to a fortune and title, like you are," Ambrose added.

"Neither," Tristram reminded him, "am I heir to a title if my brother's widow bears a male."

And if he did not restore the Bisterne jewels to the family, Tristram wouldn't continue to receive so much as the quarterly allowance owed him as the second son. Taking away Tristram's only means of support was his father's way of punishing him for failing as a military officer. Not that Tristram considered what he had done a failure. It had succeeded quite well and saved dozens of lives. Unfortunately, saving lives was not the outcome the superior officers wanted.

His body tense enough to strain the seams of his formal coat, Tristram focused a narrow-eyed glare at his cousin. "Why did you break that bow and how do you expect to replace it?"

"I'll take the train down to the city and buy a new one." Ambrose stroked the splintered edge of the bow. "It looks rather worn anyway. Miss VanDorn might appreciate something new."

"Purchased with what?" Tristram asked.

Ambrose grinned. "Your largess, cousin."

"Reward money for retrieving the jewels." Florian made the suggestion without a hint of humor.

"If she hasn't had them all copied and sold the originals." Tristram retrieved the undamaged comb from his coat pocket and held the jewels up to one of the gas sconces set on the wall.

The yellowish light glinted in the diamonds and pearls, but then the former were faceted enough that this poor form of illumination would shimmer off even cut crystal. He needed sunlight and a magnifying glass to be certain these jewels were artificial.

"The ones you found on the Continent were real. Or at least the jewelers and pawnbrokers thought so." Florian picked up the cello. "We know she must have sold those."

"But they could have been copied first." Ambrose also began to pack up the instrument he'd been using. "We'd best hurry if we wish to dance with Miss VanDorn again. She may leave at any moment, and we don't have permission to call."

Florian rose but remained motionless, as Tristram still blocked the doorway. "Our hostess can leave cards for us."

"If the elder Mrs. Selkirk is willing to do so." Tristram didn't move from the door. "I have the impression that the Selkirks and the VanDorns are not in the habit of making social calls."

"Then we should have made better arrangements." Ambrose joined Florian facing Tristram. "Are you going to get out of our way, Cousin?"

"In a moment." Tristram dropped his gaze to the fragments of the bow in Ambrose's hand. "You still haven't told me why you broke that."

Ambrose's mouth tightened at the corners, forming furrows beside his lips that added ten years to his five and twenty. "Rage. Pure and simple rage that she would steal and lie and cheat her husband, my old friend, and then the Baston-Wards, and act as though she were the affronted one."

"She is rather cool for a lady we accused of stealing a fortune in gemstones." Florian drummed his fingertips on the top of the cello's neck.

Tristram recalled seeing her ladyship drumming her fingers against her own wrist and shook his head. "Not as cool as all that. She's anxious about something."

"Being caught in her larceny." Florian grinned as though the prospect of catching her ladyship in the act of thievery pleased him. "Now, if you will excuse us, Tris, we would like to stow these instruments and then do some pursuing of our own."

Tristram stepped aside and opened the door for the other men. They moved down the hall with strides long and fast enough to fall minutely shy of a trot. He followed at a more leisurely pace, even allowing himself to get trapped behind a crowd of paunchy and balding older men who reeked of cigar smoke and talked too loudly. They reminded him of his father—wealthy, self-satisfied men who spoke of nothing but stock investments, railroads, and land. They talked of ordering this person to do this and that person to do that. How many of those minions were their sons, whom they called "Disappointments"? If any of those sons of these American equivalent of noblemen wanted to go into the church rather than order others around, they, too, would more than likely be shoved into a profession for which they were wholly unsuited, or worse, be like his brother and have no profession at all, to their own destruction.

And perhaps he was being judgmental without cause, and many of these men and their offspring wanted to do good in the world, as did Tristram. With the stipend his father promised him if he succeeded in finding the gemstones and proving he was not a ne'er-do-well embarrassment to the Wolfe family, Tristram could do a great deal of good in the world.

The steps before him cleared, and he descended two at a time. He wanted to observe Lady Catherine Bisterne before she was aware of his presence in the ballroom and see if she was as nervous without him around as she had been with him close at hand.

CHAPTER 3

"Paying visits differs from leaving cards in that you must ask to be received."
Emily Price Post

"I told Mr. Wolfe and Mr. Baston-Ward they may call on me today."
Estelle's cocoa-brown eyes sparked with golden lights behind their
fringe of long lashes. "And not for Mama's at home, with all those twit-
tering matrons gossiping and drinking tea."

Catherine set down the slice of dry toast she had barely touched
and stared at her younger sister across the breakfast table. "You can't do
that, Stell. They are penniless ne'er-do-wells who are only interested in
your trust fund."

"They are interested in my music." Estelle clipped out each word.
"Both are accomplished musicians who have no instruments on which
to practice here."

"They don't even have titles to recommend them."

Color bloomed fiery along Estelle's cheekbones. "I'd rather my friends
have only their musical ability to recommend them than someone like
your husband, who had nothing more than his title to recommend him."

The toast crumbled between Catherine's fingers, the crumbs pattering onto her plate like drops of dry rain. Tears stung her eyes and she looked away from Estelle, focused on the expanse of Tuxedo Lake toward the wooded hills, slate-gray like the sky, with white edging the wavelets in the center. A sheen of ice rimmed the shore like her heart—cold on the outside, bleak and turbulent in the center.

"You're right, Stell." Catherine's throat constricted so badly she couldn't speak above a murmur. "Edwin chose to give nothing to the world but his title, but then, that was all I thought I wanted. Well, his title and his handsome face. Which is precisely why I wish to spare you from looking only to the surface of the man."

"I know." Estelle reached across the table and covered Catherine's hand with hers. "So few people here are accomplished musicians, and Mama never lets me associate with the townspeople anymore."

"I understand they were giving you notions of joining a band." Catherine grimaced at the mere word denoting some group of lower Manhattan factory workers who turned amateur performers on their off days. "That's no life for a VanDorn."

"And what is a life for a VanDorn?" Estelle removed her hand and drummed her long fingers on the lace table runner. "A marriage where I live here and my husband stays in the city more nights than he's at home with me and the children? I do not wish to be pathetic like Mrs. Post. She drives down to the train station night after night hoping her husband will appear. And he scarcely ever does. I'm mortified for her. And then you were stranded in that mausoleum of a house on Romney Marsh, while your husband gambled away your dowry in London."

"Bisterne is a very beautiful manor house, not a mausoleum."

"After your money stopped it from crumbling to bits."

"What do you know of it?" Catherine's voice emerged louder, harsher than she intended.

Mama swept into the dining room on a cloud of lavender-and-rose perfume. "Girls, you aren't quarreling, are you?"

"No, Mama," they chorused.

"Good. Catherine created quite enough of a stir last night with wearing that mauve-and-green gown five months too early, and we don't wish to have the servants gossiping about how the two of you cannot get along with one another." Mama paused in her speech as a footman entered bearing fresh coffee steaming in a silver pot.

He drew out Mama's chair with his free hand, then poured coffee into the cup already set at her place. Mama took only black coffee for breakfast, which was probably why she remained girlishly slim despite her forty-five years. Apparently knowing this, the footman departed the room without so much as offering to fill a plate for her.

"You should have remained for the entire ball," Mama continued as though she hadn't paused while the servant was in the room. "You looked ashamed of yourself, Catherine. And Estelle, you will never find a husband if you don't allow young men to court you."

"I don't want—"

Catherine shot her a quelling glance, then faced Mama. "I had developed a headache."

"I saw old Mrs. Selkirk talking to you." Mama raised her coffee to her lips to drink and her eyebrows to query.

Catherine raised her own cup as though she and Mama saluted one another with foils before a duel—coffee cups at five paces. "I'm to stay away from Lord Tristram Wolfe."

Estelle smirked. "Which you didn't."

"He wouldn't stay away from me. In fact—" Catherine took a deep breath. She may as well get this out of the way now. "He's calling this morning."

"Indeed?" As dark a blue as Catherine's, Mama's eyes gleamed from beneath half-mast lids. "Will I be the first mama in Tuxedo Park— or Newport, for that matter—to see her daughter marry two English titles?"

"I have no intention of marrying another Englishman." Catherine pushed back her chair. "And if you want the best for your younger daughter, you will be cautious about allowing Mr. Wolfe and Mr. Baston-Ward to call upon her. They are highly unlikely to inherit titles without a number of men dying prematurely."

As her husband had—far too prematurely. No man should die a month short of his thirty-fifth birthday, but Edwin, Lord Bisterne, had never awakened after a night of excesses in dining, drinking, and gaming.

"I'm not interested in them as beaux." Estelle rose, plate in hand, and headed for the sideboard. "I wish for someone willing to indulge my love of playing good music. We will practice for an hour this morning."

Unwise of you, little sister. Catherine poised on the edge of her chair, expecting Mama to forbid such a plan.

Mama's face took on a beatific glow. "Those two nice young men you danced with last night? That sounds perfectly acceptable as a form of activity."

"But, Mama, they're—"

"Gentlemen." Mama stopped Catherine's protest. "And where would you like to meet your young man, Catherine?"

"The conservatory."

Despite the radiators, the room would be freezing with all of its windows. That might convince him to make his stay as brief as possible.

"I believe his call is purely business," she added. "At least I hope that's all. I truly do not wish to upset Mrs. Selkirk."

Mama sighed. "What did she threaten? To ruin us, I suppose?"

"Something like that."

"She hasn't managed to do so yet." Estelle returned to the table with enough ham and eggs on her plate to ensure she wouldn't keep her girlish figure for more than another six months or so. "Or not entirely."

Catherine stiffened. "What do you mean?"

"Nothing important." Estelle took a dainty bite of ham and began to chew with extensive vigor.

Mama sighed. "Estelle was uninvited to a party or two after Mrs. Selkirk learned she had been in the village playing her music with some of the workers."

"I didn't want to go to the parties anyway. Well, not all of them."

"One was a garden party with Mrs. Lorillard, the younger one." Mama blinked as though the memory brought tears to her eyes.

Catherine shot to her feet. "I will send a note around to Lord Tristram right now telling him not to come. Even if his business has to do with Bisterne's estate and not anything social, I won't risk anything bad happening to the family."

She stalked from the room and headed for the library and paper and pens.

A freshly filled fountain pen lay on the desk along with a stack of paper and envelopes. She seated herself in the wide leather chair and picked up the pen just as the clock on the mantel chimed eleven.

Of course. The hour was late. Despite leaving the ball early, Catherine hadn't slept until well after Estelle ceased playing the piano in the music room, and their parents and brother returned from the ball. The clock's four chimes had risen through the floorboards before Catherine slept, and she woke six hours later. How Papa and Paul Three managed to remain at entertainments until past midnight, then catch a train into New York in the morning, she never understood. She needed her sleep.

Now she needed to be awake, hurry with her note so a footman could carry it over to the Selkirk house on Lake Wee Wah. Now clear-headed in the cold light of day and not bemused by old Mrs. Selkirk's lingering hostility and her own poor judgment in wearing mauve satin instead of black silk, she would have remembered she could refuse a call from Lord Tristram Wolfe. Catherine, Lady Bisterne, didn't need to receive a man who had outright accused her of a crime.

The quarter hour chimed. No time now to get across the park to the other lake before Lord Tristram left.

Catherine crumpled the note and tossed it onto the embers of a banked fire. The vellum smoldered on the coals for a moment, flared in a short-lived burst of flame, then died like her brief notion that she could refuse to meet with the younger son of the Marquess of Cothbridge. If she did not, he might tell the Selkirks that he suspected her of being a thief. He might go as far as to contact local authorities, or worse, some diplomatic service between England and America. The resultant scandal would destroy Catherine and her family despite her innocence.

Many might not believe in her innocence. From stealing fiancés to stealing family heirlooms was a large step, and yet Catherine's detractors in the past might leap to that conclusion, though she had come home to mend the past, not create more scandals. She must silence Lord Tristram, allay his suspicions.

She must keep Estelle from igniting the smoke signals of scandal by indulging her music with two young men, two strangers, two gentlemen who were twice removed from inheriting titles—or anything at all.

Catherine, the Dowager Countess of Bisterne, a thief indeed. She had taken Georgette's fiancé, but that was different from heirloom jewelry. Fiancés could be replaced. Why Georgette had not done so was something Catherine must find out, if she could make her meeting with Lord Tristram brief.

"Stolen jewels indeed." With more vigor than was strictly ladylike, Catherine climbed the flaring staircase to the second floor and her bedchamber. As did every room in the house, her room faced the lake. Nodding to her maid, who perched on a stool by the radiator, Catherine strode to the window. She rubbed frost from the glass and gazed at the water. The waves in the center frothed like her insides. She should have eaten. She should have thought to send the man packing earlier. She should have . . .

Too many "should haves" filled her life. Her homecoming was supposed to remove as many of those from her past as possible; therefore, she would start with Lord Tristram Wolfe.

Chilled away from the heat, she paced across the carpet with its blousy, pink rose pattern, and stopped at her dressing table. Smelling faintly of magnolia scent, her jewel case, red velvet with her initials picked out in diamond chips on the lid, rested atop the golden wood. The bottom drawer held the other jewels Bisterne had given her during their marriage, pieces he declared were not part of the family set. Considering he had lied about the hair combs, she doubted she could trust his word on these either, or even believe they were real jewels at all. She pulled a string of amber beads out of the box and held them up to the light. Despite the grayness of the day, the beads glowed in light from the gaslights and warmed in her hand. Artificial amber, if it existed, could not do this. Nor could plastic like that ghastly yellow handbag her maid, Sapphire, carried.

Catherine laid the beads on the dressing table and pulled out a brooch with a ruby surrounded by pearls. "Sapphire?"

"Yes, my lady?" The lady's maid glanced up.

"You were a lady's maid for twenty years before you came to work for me, were you not?"

"Twenty-two, yes, my lady." Sapphire's dark gray eyes narrowed. "Is there a problem with the quality of my work?"

"Not at all. I was thinking perhaps you know a great deal about jewels." Catherine held the ruby toward the light. "Is this real or paste?"

Sapphire's eyes widened. "My Lord Bisterne gave that to you."

Catherine said nothing.

"It's beautiful, my lady, and will look fine against that blue silk you had made up at Worth's in Paris."

Catherine ran her thumbnail across a pearl, wondering if Sapphire would think her stark staring mad if she tried to bite one of the gemstones to see if it gave that gritty feeling only true pearls exhibited.

She did not need to discover whether these gemstones were real. She would return them to the Earl of Bisterne—eventually.

She started to replace the amber beads and ruby brooch in her jewel case. "If I dare wear—"

A knock sounded on the door. Catherine jumped and jabbed the pin of the brooch into her thumb. She didn't need to open the door to know a footman stood beyond it to tell her Lord Tristram had arrived.

While she wrapped her bleeding thumb in a handkerchief, Sapphire answered the door. Lord Tristram had indeed arrived on the stroke of eleven thirty. Catherine nodded assent that she would receive him and unwrapped her thumb. Only a few drops of blood marred the whiteness of the black-bordered linen, but the digit throbbed too much for gloves to be comfortable.

"It's morning. It's my parents' home. I won't look improperly dressed." She spoke the excuses aloud as she patted a stray tendril of hair back into place before the mirror.

The reflection of her diamond engagement ring and wedding band winked back at her. She dropped her hand and stared at the diamond-crusted circlets in horror. Those rings were most definitely Baston-Ward heirlooms. Her husband had made that clear on their wedding day. Catherine never removed them from her hand, had not for five years. Going into muted colors after only a year and a month was one way to announce her widowhood, but removing the engagement ring and wedding ring band was quite another statement, a declaration that she would accept advances from other gentlemen, which she could not. Yet how could she walk down the corridor and declare her innocence to Lord Tristram Wolfe when she did indeed wear jewelry that did not belong to her?

∽

Tristram walked from the Selkirks' large but neat imitation Elizabethan house to the VanDorn Lake House. He hoped the exercise and biting air would ease the tension gripping his innards. Neither succeeded. By the time he climbed the steps to the fascinating curved edifice of the building with the unimaginative name of Lake House, his guts felt as though they had turned into watch springs.

He pressed the doorbell, then stood drumming his fingers against his thighs. A second before the door opened, he remembered to remove a calling card to hand to the silver-haired butler.

"Lord Tristram Wolfe." The man read from the pasteboard. "Her ladyship is expecting you."

Tristram followed the man's straight back across a corridor that curved gently away from the door. Several rooms opened along the hall's length, and a stairway swooped from the middle. He expected the butler to show him into one of these rooms—parlor, library, even a cozy sitting room perhaps. Instead, the man headed up the staircase, pausing where it widened into a landing.

"Make yourself comfortable, my lord. Lady Bisterne will be with you shortly." The butler bowed and withdrew.

Tristram stared at the panorama before him. The chamber stood out from the first—no, Americans called this the second—floor of the house to allow floor-to-ceiling windows on three sides. The abundance of glass made for a chilly chamber despite two radiators. But the view made up for the cold. Beyond the floor-to-ceiling glass, the wind whipped up the waters of the lake against a backdrop of the woods. Between the lake and house, gardens lay dormant, and a gazebo that would be attractive in warmer months was poised beneath a shelter of oaks with spreading branches. The house itself was the most spectacular sight as its structure curved to accommodate the line of the water.

"Astounding." The word escaped his lips as footfalls tapped behind him on the stone floor.

"It is, rather."

He startled at the sound of her voice. With the background of orchestra and chattering voices the night before, he had not heard her accent with clarity. Somehow, he expected her to sound English, or like an American trying to sound English, as was usually the situation with Americans who had married Englishmen. But she spoke with the restrained accent of a privileged Yankee like everyone he had met at the ball.

Half smiling at his own foolishness, he faced her ladyship and held out his hand. "Thank you for receiving me, Lady Bisterne."

"Of course." She accepted his proffered hand.

Her fingers felt like icicles against his palm, and for a moment, he fought the urge to clasp her hand in his and warm it. The action would give him a moment to gaze at her by the light of day, for she was worth a moment or a hundred of gazing.

She'd been pretty last night by the gaslights of the clubhouse. Even in the gray of today, her complexion glowed like a natural pearl, emphasizing the depth of her dark eyes behind lashes long and thick enough they shouldn't be real, but more than likely were. The dark green jacket and skirt she wore brought out red lights in her smooth hair. All of her was smooth, neat perfection except for that cleft in her chin. That dimple, that slip of the sculptor's chisel, served to emphasize the flawlessness of her bones, while making her far more approachable, far more . . . appealing. Too appealing.

No wonder Bisterne had fallen for her. The wonder was how he had managed to leave her behind at Bisterne while he cavorted in London.

His mouth suddenly dry, Tristram tucked his thumbs into the pockets of his coat and forced his gaze from Catherine to a suite of sofas and chairs resting upon a Persian carpet in the center of the room. "May we be seated? This may take a while."

"I will send for coffee." Her nostrils pinched. "Or would you prefer tea?"

He would. Perhaps the VanDorn cook made better tea than did the Selkirks', but her face told him she disliked that oh-so-English beverage. "Coffee is well enough."

While she rang for a footman to bring up coffee, Tristram returned his attention to the lake. The waves had died down, and precipitation suspiciously resembling snow drifted down like feathers from a burst pillow. "Snow at the beginning of November."

"Not uncommon here. They've been seeing a little bit here and there since the middle of October."

He glanced over his shoulder. Seeing she had seated herself on a sofa facing the bank of side windows, he headed for the seating area and settled on a chair across from her. "They? You weren't here?"

"I only arrived in Tuxedo Park three days ago." She plucked a bit of lint from her skirt. "From Dieppe."

"Dieppe? Wouldn't Le Havre have been more convenient?"

Her hands flattened on the brown velvet cushion, and a stillness settled over her. "I traveled by the private yacht of some family friends. But how do you know where I was in France?" Her voice clipped out as cold and brittle as the ice rimming the edge of the lake.

"I thought I would—"

The arrival of coffee, hot and fragrant, along with cream, sugar, and sweet biscuits, interrupted him. Her question and his partial response hovered in the air like a hawk ready to dive onto its prey while she thanked the footman, then poured Tristram coffee, adding the dollop of cream and pinch of sugar he requested in answer to her query. Not until she had settled back on the sofa, a fragile china cup cradled in her hands, did he continue.

"I thought I could catch up with you in Paris, and then Le Havre, but I miscalculated the direction there and arrived in New York a week ahead of you."

Her eyes widened a little too far for genuine surprise. "Why, may I ask, were you following me?"

"To recover the jewels, of course." He smiled.

She gave him a blank stare, sipped coffee, then set the cup on the low table between them. Light from the wall sconces flashed off the diamond-studded wedding band and matching engagement ring on her left hand, rings that should grace the far-less-attractive fingers of the current Countess of Bisterne, Florian's sister-in-law.

Tristram leaned forward and slipped his hand beneath Lady Catherine Bisterne's fingers and tilted them so a cold flame burned at the heart of the engagement diamond. "Shall we start with these rings?"

CHAPTER 4

"A handshake often creates a feeling of liking or of irritation between two strangers. Who does not dislike a 'boneless' hand extended as though it were a spray of sea-weed, or a miniature boiled pudding? It is equally annoying to have one's hand clutched aloft in grotesque affectation and shaken violently sideways, as though it were being used to clean a spot out of the atmosphere. What woman does not wince at the viselike grasp that cuts her rings into her flesh and temporarily paralyzes every finger?" Emily Price Post

Blood drained from Catherine's face. Beneath Tristram's gripping fingers, the rings warmed. Her eyes squeezed shut, and her lips, no longer deep pink, compressed.

"Please." Her voice rasped barely above a whisper, and she tugged her hand free.

Tristram considered rising and crossing the room so he could bang his head against one of the myriad glass panes in the windows to knock some sense into himself. She hadn't just been reacting in guilt; he had been holding her hand too tightly.

"I am sorry, my lady." An urge to raise her hand to his lips washed over him. If blood had drained from her face, then it surely washed into his, for his ears and cheeks burned. His necktie grew too tight. "I forgot myself."

"I'd ask you to leave, but I believe we have unfinished business." Her hands steady, her expression the smooth mask adopted by any lady used to court circles, she refilled both their coffee cups. Instead of picking up hers, she twisted the rings off her finger and laid them on the table, where the diamonds winked and shimmered like lighthouse beacons warning of danger ahead. "As you can see, I have never taken them off." Her ring finger bore the marks of rings long worn. "I was afraid to remove them lest people think I was hunting for another husband." Two rapid blinks betrayed emotion trying to break through her façade. "I'd recommend you tell old Mrs. Selkirk that, but then you would have to admit you were here."

"I expect she already knows." He seized on the diversion like a man stuck in quicksand grasping a rope to haul him out. "I had to ask the Selkirk butler for directions here."

"They wouldn't lend you their carriage?"

"I wanted to walk."

This time, the widening of her eyes was natural surprise. "You wanted to walk in this cold?"

She glanced at the windows. Beyond the glass, snow swirled like a million ballerinas intending to defy gravity and never touch the ground. What flakes did land melted on impact, leaving the winter-brown grass and the walkways to gazebo and lake merely wet and not coated in cleansing white.

"After two years in South Africa," Tristram said, "I appreciate precipitation regardless of its temperature."

"You were in South Africa?" She gave him a look of sincere interest.

He returned it with a rueful shrug. "Not a shining hour of mine. The Boer War."

"That's right. I remember hearing something about your being in the military. You—" She pressed her fingers to her lips as though trying to shove back the rest of her thought.

He bowed his head. "Captain Lord Tristram Wolfe at your service, my lady."

Except he didn't have a true right to use the military rank. He hoped she didn't recall that bit of gossip she must have heard even immured at Bisterne there on the edge of Romney Marsh. He had, after all, been allowed to resign his commission rather than disgrace the family with a court-martial.

"But since I resigned"—he hastened to emphasize this fact—"I never use the rank."

"You were wounded." Her glance flicked to his head. "Are you certain you're quite well?"

His hand flew to the top of his head, where his hat had failed to flatten the cowlick, and he narrowed his eyes at her. "Are you suggesting that my conviction that you are responsible for the missing Bisterne jewels is a result of my being bashed on the head?"

"I would never be so vulgar."

"You're wearing colors. The vulgarity of that was all Mrs. Selkirk talked of at breakfast this morning."

Catherine laughed.

An invisible hand wound the already taut watch springs of Tristram's middle. He drank his now cold coffee in an attempt to ease the tension inside him.

"Shall I order fresh coffee so we may start this conversation over, Lord Tristram?" Catherine rose without waiting for his response and crossed the room to the bell. "My sister tells me she is trying to convince our father that telephones in each room and not simply the front hall will save the servants a great deal of work running up and down steps, as they can be set up so we could call them with our request. But then, Estelle likes gadgets. She is forever recording her own music on her phonograph cylinders. I prefer to listen to live music myself, and perhaps one day—"

The arrival of the footman stopped the uninterrupted string of chatter. She gave the order for fresh coffee and remained silent until the footman removed the tray of used cups, his stare fixed on the discarded rings the whole time he gathered up china and silver. The instant the man's footfalls no longer sounded on the stair treads, Tristram rather expected her ladyship to take up her flow of chatter where she had left off. Instead, she glided across the room to a set of windows, her soft wool skirt flowing around her like dark green water ending an inch or two above the floor.

"Enough fencing, my Lord Tristram." She spoke with her back to him, though the day had grown so dark with cloud cover her reflection shone in the glass. "So tell me, what transformed you from soldier to Scotland Yard detective? Tell me why you and my cousin by marriage have accused me of stealing jewels from the Bisterne estate. Other than the wedding and engagement ring, of course. That was an accident. I never thought about how they belonged to the estate until this morning before your call. Surely you didn't chase me across Europe because of a couple of paltry rings."

Paltry? The new Earl of Bisterne could feed every tenant on his estate for a year with the price of those rings alone.

Tristram said nothing for a full minute before he rose and joined her at the window. "I'm scarcely a Scotland Yard detective, my lady. We have a family connection to the current Lord Bisterne, and his father was a friend of my father's from the time they were in short pants until Baston-Ward's death a half-dozen years ago. Baston-Ward made some foolish investments many years ago that decimated his fortune, and his son tried to recoup those losses through gaming instead of hard work."

"A trait of the family," Catherine murmured.

Tristram inclined his head in acknowledgement. "Which is why the estate fell into such disrepair."

"It isn't in disrepair now, thanks to my dowry." A hint of bitterness edged her tone.

Tristram barely managed to stop himself from reaching out and touching her hand, her elbow, her face in a gesture of comfort. She had made her bed. If Edwin, Lord Bisterne, had not been such a profligate in gaming, drink, and food consumption, she would still be lying in that bed of neglect after buying her way into the English nobility. Surely she had known the risks, but then, perhaps she had not. She couldn't have been above eighteen or nineteen years of age when she had succumbed to the lure of a title and Bisterne's charm.

"You gave a number of people much needed work." He offered truth for comfort.

"But that won't last. The dowry reverted back to my trust-fund principal upon my husband's death."

"Which is where the jewels come in. Bisterne needs to sell them to gain capital enough to continue the estate into a paying prospect."

The footman returned with a chime of silver and rattle of china. Tristram and Catherine stared out the window. The snow had turned to freezing rain that pattered against the glass like ballerinas metamorphosed into vaudeville tap dancers.

The footman departed, and in his wake rose the soaring notes of a violin.

"That's not Ambrose playing."

"That is Estelle. We don't know where she gets her talent. Mama and even my father and brother can play adequately at the piano, but Estelle's talent is something special."

"I hear that."

She was playing Vivaldi with a warmth that probably would have pleased the composer. It pleased Tristram, cutting straight to his heart as good music should. With those glorious notes swooping up the staircase, discussing the larceny of the musician's sister seemed just as much a crime as taking someone else's jewelry.

"My lady." His throat felt tight. "I didn't believe my father when he told me the Bisterne jewels were missing and you were the only person who could have taken them. But when he commissioned me to do so, I set out to follow you anyway."

"Why would your father commission such a duty?"

"For the sake of his lifelong friend, your late husband's father. Apparently, Bisterne saved my father's life when they were callow youths."

"How honorable of him to go to such . . . trouble." Her tone was dry.

Tristram understood she meant "expense" rather than "trouble" but was too polite to ask who had paid for this expense. The answer was simple—his father, of course. Tristram was still a younger son unless his sister-in-law gave birth to a girl. Tristram had little money of his own. She would guess that, and his next words would tell her his father had gone to a great deal of expense on behalf of the Earl of Bisterne.

"I found too much evidence to deny his charges against you."

"Besides the wedding and engagement rings?" Her voice was as expressionless as the side of her face he could see.

"Considerably more." He was growing numb standing so close to the expanse of glass. "Shall we sit?" He could see her better if they faced one another across a coffee service than side by side staring into the autumnal gloom.

Wordlessly, she returned to the sofa, touched her fingertips to the side of the coffeepot, and poured them fresh cups. He sat, then took his cup. Neither of them drank. They sat in identical poses, their backs too straight to touch the cushions behind them, their gazes fixed somewhere beyond the other's shoulders, their hands seeking warmth from the cups.

Then Catherine blinked twice and met his eyes in a challenge. "So what is this evidence?"

"You spent the past thirteen months in Italy and France." He drew up a mental list. "Venice, Rome, and Florence. Avignon, Lyon, and

Paris. In each of those cities, I found at least one piece of jewelry where it had been sold to a local jeweler."

✆

A lifetime of training kept Catherine's face stiff, her teeth clenched together. If she opened her mouth for so much as a sip of coffee, she would probably shriek with hysterical laughter or say something unforgivably rude to Tristram.

He shifted on his chair, set down his cup, and drew a sheaf of papers from an inside pocket of his coat. "Receipts." He held them out to her. "For the pieces I managed to recover."

She snatched the receipts from him and scanned prices in lire, then francs. Each bill of purchase was attached to a detailed description and drawing.

"Who made these?" She tapped on a picture.

"They were in the vault where the jewels should have been."

"I never saw them there."

"So you did go into the vault?"

She slapped the papers onto the sofa beside her. "Of course I did. I was mistress of the house. We kept coin there for paying workmen and wages on quarter days. When Bisterne was rarely at home, that duty fell to me more often than not. I never even saw most of the jewelry. Other than a parure of emeralds, I never even wore any of the jewelry. It wasn't to my taste."

"And the combs."

"Those were a wedding gift." To her horror, tears filled her eyes. She blinked, but to no avail. The tears puddled on her lower lids. "And you know they are artificial. Perhaps they all are."

Tristram shifted on his chair, glanced at her face, away, and back again. Finally, he produced a white linen handkerchief and leaned forward to press it into her hand. "None of them, according to the jewelers, are artificial. And in thirteen months, you had plenty of time to have copies made."

"I wouldn't wear paste gemstones." She dashed the handkerchief across her eyes, then crushed it between her fingers. "I think you need to leave, my lord. You have been here long enough, and my intentions are to make amends with Georgette Selkirk, not make matters worse between our families." She rose to force him to do so.

He was too well-bred not to, but he gave her an uncompromising stare, pinned her with the intensity of eyes nearly as dark as her walking suit. "No one else had the opportunity, the access to the jewels except for you and Edwin. But Edwin was already gone, so that leaves you. Added to the jewels found along your route through Europe, and I know I will find a way to prove you have or know where to find the rest."

"You may try, my lord, but you are forgetting one important detail."

"Indeed?"

"Why would I do such a thing? My quarterly allowance from my trust fund holds more money than all the Bisterne jewels put together."

For a heartbeat, his eyes flickered, a veritable shriek of uncertainty. Then he smiled and bowed. "*Touché*, my lady, but I will find my motivation."

"You are welcome to try, Mr. Holmes."

He laughed at her calling him after Sir Arthur Conan Doyle's famous detective, just as Ambrose had. "I will find a reason, my lady. I likely have more of a stake in winning this game than do you." He executed the most fluid and graceful bow she had witnessed since her husband's death, then he clasped her hand in his and raised her fingers to his lips.

A jolt of electricity shot through her, and she snatched her hand away. "How dare you?" The words emerged in a croak rather than the hauteur she wished.

"With very little trouble." He smiled, turned so smartly on his heels she expected him to salute the portrait of her grandfather hanging at the top of the steps, then strode from the room.

Once he had descended the steps far enough that he couldn't look through the railings and see her, Catherine sank onto the sofa. She started to lower her head to cover her face with her hands until she regained her composure—and spotted the rings still lying on the table.

Not as confident as he pretended. He wouldn't have forgotten the rings if he were.

"He can do without them."

Yet those were legitimately within his milieu to take from her on behalf of the new Lord Bisterne. They never should have left England on her finger. She could have purchased a plain gold band to let the world know she was not in the market for a second spouse.

No help for it—she needed to catch him up and give him the rings. He would not find more reasons to accuse her of being a jewel thief.

She snatched up band and betrothal diamond, and with them clutched in her fist she raced down the steps to the entryway. It stood stark and empty, cold stone lighted by long windows on either side of the front door.

She flung open that door and gazed down the path leading through the trees to the road. Snow fell again, tumbling in sheets that clung to the sparkle of ice upon the grass and flagstones. If Lord Tristram were out there, she could not see him. If she tried to follow, she would likely slip and fall in her light leather shoes, not to mention how she would freeze in her thin wool jacket and lace-trimmed shirtwaist.

Already shivering, she shut the door, headed for the nearest fire, and heard the music recommence. It was a cello this time, an instrument Estelle hadn't mastered as well as she liked. The cellist here had mastered it.

"Florian." Catherine sprinted for the music room door as though the corridor were a tennis court and she needed to catch the ball.

She yanked open the door. The music stuttered to a halt. Estelle spun around on the piano stool to glare at Catherine. And three gentlemen stood, two with instruments and bows in hand. The third held nothing but a top hat.

No wonder Lord Tristram had managed to disappear from the foyer and lane so quickly. He hadn't left the house at all.

She closed the door and leaned against it to support her suddenly wobbly legs.

"Don't tell us to stop." Estelle widened her eyes in entreaty. "This piece was just coming together."

"Your sister is a wonderful composer, Lady Bisterne." Florian gave Estelle a look of pure devotion.

"Estelle, a composer?" Catherine shook her head. Her neck cracked, shooting a pain through her skull. She raised her hand to rub the taut muscles and remembered the rings she still clutched. "I'd like to hear it, but at the moment, Lord Tristram forgot something."

"We were just about to play it for Lord Tristram." Estelle faced the piano and rested her hands on the keyboard. "I call this 'Praise.'"

Praise indeed. For the next ten minutes, the music rose to the heavens, a complete distraction from anything but a reminder that Catherine had spent too little time in praise and thankfulness over the past five years. Or perhaps in her life. Though far from perfect, with the men having just learned the melody, the instruments sang and drove the tune into her heart.

When the last note quivered from the room, the five of them remained silent and still, everyone seeming to hold his or her breath so as not to miss a decibel.

The chime of the doorbell broke the stillness. The three musicians expelled their breaths and exchanged smiles of congratulations. On the far side of the room, Lord Tristram bowed to Estelle. "A not-so-subtle reminder of what so rarely falls from our lips."

"If we had a poet who could write lyrics," Florian began.

"And a voice capable of singing them to this music," Ambrose added.

"We could make a fortune singing this for—"

"I'm a lady." Estelle's upper lip curled as her sarcastic tones interrupted Florian's enthusiasm. "I don't perform for anyone other than my own kind."

"A waste," Lord Tristram murmured.

"Do not," Catherine bit out, "encourage her. That is, don't encourage her to become a performer. One scandal in the family is more than enough."

And there she did it—reminded Lord Tristram of her elopement to Edwin, Lord Bisterne, and consequently the missing jewels.

To distract them all, she skirted Ambrose and Florian and rested her hand on Estelle's shoulder. "I'll make a bargain with you, baby sister. If you promise to attend all the social events Mama wishes you to attend, I will see to it you may practice as much of the rest of the time as you like."

"With Mr. Wolfe and Mr. Baston-Ward?" Estelle looked up with shining eyes. "Truly?"

"Yes, truly. But do please ask Sapphire or one of the other maids to be in here with you in the future." Catherine squeezed the delicate shoulder beneath her hand. "A deal?"

"A deal." Estelle shot to her feet and enveloped Catherine in an embrace. "I don't care what anyone says about you. You always were the best sister a girl could have."

"Wait until the holiday season of parties is over before you make those kinds of declarations." Catherine kept her tone stern, but her heart swelled.

Then Lord Tristram strode up to them, and the rings seemed to catch fire inside her fist. Slowly, painfully, she forced her fingers open and held out her hand, the rings gleaming dully in the snowy light.

"Thank you." He removed the rings from her palm without touching her. "Now to get the rest back."

"I have no idea how you will do that." Catherine lifted her chin. "I have no idea where they are. Nor do I care. The rings were a thoughtless action, and I'm happy you're taking away my last reminder—I do apologize, Florian, but the truth here is necessary—of a man to whom I was a good and faithful wife, and who broke nearly every one of our marriage vows. I no longer want a reminder of my greatest mistake."

"Thank you for saying so, my lady." Tristram tucked the rings into his pocket. "You have just given me a missing piece in this puzzle."

"Motivation for taking the jewels." As Ambrose spoke, he looked as satisfied as a cat who'd been locked into the dairy.

CHAPTER 5

"When Mrs. Gilding returns he says, 'Mr. Blank telephoned he would not be able to come for dinner as he was called to Washington. Mr. Bachelor will be happy to come in his place.'" Emily Price Post

She had given Tristram—all three of them—a motivation for her to steal the Bisterne jewels: revenge. Catherine read it in the satisfaction on Ambrose's face before he and Florian voiced it aloud.

A dozen protests to her innocence rose to her lips. She suppressed them all. When she was an adolescent roaming a little too freely around the newly developed Tuxedo Park and denied getting up to some mischief with her friends, Papa reminded her that she could not prove a negative unless she possessed a good alibi. He, however, with little work, could prove her guilt, so she may as well either produce the alibi or confess.

In this event, she possessed no alibi. Nor could she prove the negative that she had not taken the jewels. She could only find a way to prove her innocence.

Or the guilt of someone else.

"Believe what you like, my lord. I will prove you wrong." She gave him a direct, challenging glare.

He met it, and sparks crackled between them as though she had been playing the childhood game of sliding across a carpet in stockinged feet and trying to touch Paul Three or Estelle and create the satisfying snap. Sometimes those snaps hurt. This one gave her a jolt of power as though she were an incandescent light.

He stepped back as though he felt it, too. "I should be going." A huskiness roughened the clarity of his oh-so-English voice. "The Selkirks are expecting me for luncheon."

"Do stay here, my lord, all of you. I believe we are having broiled grapefruit salad." Estelle rose from the piano stool. "I will tell the cook to expect three more."

"Thank you, no." Tristram headed for the door.

"I will send for the carriage." Catherine hastened to beat Estelle to the bell. "The auto will never be able to drive in this snow."

"Neither is necessary, Lady Bisterne." Tristram yanked open the door, stepped over the threshold, and was gone, not awaiting the butler to show him out the front.

"He must have forgotten his manners in Cape Town." Florian touched his bow to the cello strings. "Do we have time to play a bit more before luncheon?"

"The invitation to which we will happily accept." Ambrose set aside his violin and picked up Estelle's banjo. "Will you show us how this works, Miss VanDorn?"

"The banjo? It's a lady's instrument, at least it is here. I believe in the South, the men play it. But if you like . . ." Estelle swept across the room, skirt flaring with the speed of her movement, and took possession of the banjo.

Catherine left them to it. Finding a maid replenishing the fire in the dining room, she asked her to tell the cook two gentlemen would be joining them for luncheon, and then to go sit as chaperone in the music room. That duty complete, Catherine climbed the steps to the second floor and Mama's boudoir.

She found her parent seated at her desk with a pile of invitations spilling over in front of her and a frown furrowing her brow. "What do you think of this new fashion of ringing people up to invite them to dinner?"

"I think it lacks elegance." Catherine breathed in the familiar and comforting scent of lavender and roses from Mama's perfume and a Chinese bowl of potpourri presiding on the mantel. "It is also awkward if one of the parties doesn't have a telephone."

"True, very true. The Kanes don't have one and are likely never to install one." Mama began to address one more envelope. "But this is so time-consuming and tedious. If I used the telephone, I could have Sims do all the calling."

Catherine smiled at the notion of their aging butler calling each prospective guest as though bestowing a great favor upon them. "Do all these guests have telephones?"

Mama consulted her list. "I do believe they do. This is a smallish dinner party, rather informal. More an excuse for us ladies to gather discreetly and discuss the annual Christmas tea to raise money for gifts for some of the poorer children in the village."

"That's a lovely idea." Catherine settled herself on a lavender-and-cream striped sofa. "May I assist you?"

"I would like nothing better, but surely you have friends to call on or shopping excursions in the city to arrange?"

Catherine looked down at her hands folded in her lap, covering her denuded left hand with her right. "I did more than enough shopping in France and Italy to last another year or two. And as for friends . . ." Her throat closed. "I rather scuttled those relationships when I eloped with Georgette's fiancé."

Mama sighed and returned her pen to its holder. "That was five years ago. It's past time everyone forgot about your youthful folly."

"I think they would have if Georgette had married someone else."

"And she should have. She's pretty and quite dear."

"And everyone likes her."

"Everyone likes you, too, my dear."

"Everyone liked me." Catherine emphasized the past tense. "But I apparently hurt Georgette more than I thought I had."

"Hmph." Mama brought her fist down on her desk. "And what about Lord Bisterne's behavior? He made a promise to her and broke it. Why does everyone blame my daughter as though you abducted him to the altar?"

Catherine's heart warmed at Mama's never-failing loyalty. "I did flirt with him outrageously. You told me to stop."

"But if he truly cared for Georgette, no amount of flirtation would have swayed him to run off with you. But he discovered that we have twice the money the Selkirks have, and we all knew that's all he wanted from either of you girls."

"Which is why you and Papa forbade me to so much as allow him to call." Catherine gave Mama a rueful smile. "Why do we so rarely listen to our parents when we're young?"

"You don't believe they're right. Paul Three has spared us from that sort of behavior." Mama's expression grew wistful. "He's a good son, but so very dull."

Catherine laughed. "He is that."

"Estelle, on the other hand," Mama continued, "is about to follow in your footsteps if we're not careful."

"I thought she'd have learned her lesson with me for an example, but you are so right, Mama, in more ways than one."

"Those young men in the music room are fortune hunters as well?"

"And not even the dubious honor of bearing a title."

"The title," Mama enunciated in clipped accents, "is something that spares you from ostracism here, you know, so don't dismiss its importance."

Catherine grimaced.

"But you say these young men have neither money nor title prospects?"

"Neither. But if I may offer you some advice from my own experience, don't deny her access to them. I believe now that if I had been allowed to spend more time in Bisterne's company, I would have learned his pious talk and fine manners covered an empty soul."

"And what of these young men? Are they also empty souls?"

"I don't know about Florian. His family spent most of their time in London. For all I know, he ran with my husband's set. As for Ambrose Wolfe?" Catherine wrinkled her nose. "He most definitely ran with my husband's set, though I must admit he seems to have steadied in this past year. He wasn't drinking spirits last night."

A year of Lord Tristram Wolfe's influence? As if she had reason to believe the Marquess of Cothbridge's younger son was any less profligate than her husband had been.

Mama sifted her fingers through the stack of engraved invitations. "I will discuss your suggestion with Paul tonight. We don't like this notion Estelle has of joining a band, of all things. As if a girl of good birth would ever do such a thing. I'm happy enough to have her perform at our amateur performances here, but in public? Out of the question."

"It is, and yet her talent is special. Did you know she wrote a composition she calls 'Praise'? That should not be kept inside the walls of our music room."

"She did play it for us." Mama's face glowed, smooth and lovely in the lamplight. "We pray her good sense will anchor her in doing the right thing with her music."

"Did you hope my good sense would persuade me to make the right choices?" She barely stopped herself from emitting a vulgar snort.

"I'm afraid we did, but worldliness got hold of you." Mama leaned forward and covered Catherine's clasped hands with one of hers. "Have the hardships you've endured these past five years changed that?"

"If you mean have I developed a conscience, yes." Catherine avoided meeting Mama's eyes. "I need to find a lot of forgiveness here, but Mrs. Caroline Selkirk says I will not be received, and Georgette will not speak with me."

"Then Georgette will be in the wrong, not you. As long as you conduct yourself with impeccable behavior, and we can keep Estelle from running off to join professional musicians, your being home can finally set that old scandal of yours behind us where it belongs."

Catherine flinched at Mama's kindly meant words. If she, Catherine, could not prove her innocence to Lord Tristram, a new scandal could damage her family right to its core. Estelle would never find a decent man to marry her, the sister of a jewel thief, and other men might refuse to do business with Papa and Paul Three, thus ruining the family financially. A family that had given her far too much in love, forgiveness, and money all her life deserved better than that.

Whatever course of action was necessary, she would take it to protect her family.

∞

Tristram needed the walk through the biting cold to calm him before he felt ready for a civilized meal with the Selkirks. Never in his life had a female set his blood boiling as did Lady Catherine Bisterne. She may as well have been holding a rapier in salute before an old-fashioned duel with that last glance of hers. He half expected to find himself bleeding. American-born or not, she could have given any duchess a run for her money in the hauteur division.

Suddenly he laughed, letting his voice ring out along the empty road lined with trees that hid the opulent houses beyond. She might have been nervous around him last night, but today she had herself well in hand, and the result was . . .

Alarmingly charming.

Tristram shoved his hands into the pockets of his coat. The wedding band slipped onto the tip of his finger, but could go no farther. As he paced up the hill to the Selkirk cottage, he rubbed the ring between forefinger and thumb. It was a heavy band for fingers as slender as Catherine's. The diamonds weren't set into channels, but rose over the edges of the band in a way that must have abraded her other fingers. Not a comfortable ring to wear for five years, and yet she hadn't removed it when she could have exchanged it for a plain gold band without receiving any censure. She had taken these valuable rings from the estate by her own admission. Added to the fact she was the only person at Bisterne with access to the safe at the time of her husband's death, then the fact that he had found items of the missing jewelry in her wake across Europe, and he held three powerful pieces of evidence. But figuring out a motive was even more precious.

Yet if she was guilty, would she not hand over the rest of the jewels before the truth emerged and created a scandal? The strength of her protestations of innocence pointed to her telling the truth. According to old lady Selkirk, Catherine's elopement five years earlier had created such a scandal, a handful of families, including the Selkirks, avoided the VanDorns whenever possible. Now, with Estelle to launch into society, another scandal could damage her chances of making a good match. Worse, revelation that Catherine was not the kind and trustworthy lady her family thought she was would damage, even ruin, the affection he had witnessed between the sisters.

His conscience pricked him, and he paused to gaze back down the hill toward the VanDorns' beautiful Lake House. Just the chimneys showed above the trees, so dense were the branches. He smelled the smoke from the fires sharp and tangy in the brisk air. Hearth and home, a family that seemed to care about one another, unlike his, and he could tear it apart.

"Yet what choice do I have?"

If only the fortunes of the Baston-Wards mattered in this pursuit, Tristram wouldn't care so much. They were nearly penniless due to their own mismanagement and poor behavior. But many others not at fault would suffer if the family lost a way to restore their fortune. They employed dozens of people on the estate, and almost all of them would lose their jobs. If they weren't working, tradesmen in the village would make less money supplying them with their needs. They in turn would be able to buy less . . . And so the destruction of a parish began. Similar events had taken place all over England and the Continent, as those with land lived beyond their means, made bad investments, and gambled away once-great fortunes. Money from American heiresses had saved many an estate and the jobs of the local people. Catherine's money had made improvements at Bisterne, but now it departed with her, and the jewels were all the family possessed.

"She just needs to give the Baston-Wards the money she received for the jewels and return the rest of them." His frustration burst forth in words spoken aloud to the last snowflakes still drifting to the ground, then he looked up and addressed the rest to the sky. "What else can I do but make her admit the truth?"

Silence met him, broken only by some American bird species he didn't recognize from its call. Too much silence when he cried out in anguish over not knowing which choice to make. Silence had ruled his life since the day he listened to his heart and found himself facing a court-martial for disobeying orders. Had he obeyed them, those orders would have seen dozens of innocent people killed. Of course that was the right choice. He would face that court-martial even now if he had to repeat those moments of decision. This situation, however, presented him with choices that would give him financial security such as a younger son rarely enjoyed, while helping others, and that self-interest blurred the lines between right and wrong.

Hearing the *putt-putt-putt* of an approaching motorcar and growing cold standing still, Tristram stepped to the side of the road and recommenced his climb to the Selkirk house. Georgette and Pierce expected him to be at luncheon. They wanted to discuss some activity or other they were planning, a day trip into New York. It sounded like a pleasant activity. Perhaps he could spend an extra day and investigate the finer jewelers. Meanwhile, Georgette and Pierce were comfortable companions, even if Pierce and his grandmother made clear that they would like a match between Tristram and Georgette.

The idea had crossed Tristram's mind once or twice since he'd met the pretty and gentle-spirited Georgette. An American heiress would solve a number of problems for Tristram.

If only looking into her sky-blue eyes made him feel as though he were standing at the foot of an oak during a thunderstorm. Perhaps he could change that with more time in her company.

With that in mind, he increased his speed and reached the Selkirks' at a trot. Their butler led him into the dining room, where luncheon was already underway.

"I do apologize for my tardiness." He seated himself at the last place setting. "I tarried along the road."

"Couldn't they be bothered to send a carriage with you?" The elder Mrs. Selkirk thudded her water glass onto the table. "They have no manners for all they are among the first families of New York. Georgette is much more refined than the VanDorn daughters, and she is only the second generation of heiresses."

Blushing, Georgette passed a basket of rolls to Tristram. "We'll have hot soup for you momentarily. You look half frozen."

"I like the cold." Tristram smiled at her, and she blushed more deeply.

"Don't know why you had to go down to Lake House as it is," Mrs. Selkirk the elder continued.

"Nor do you need to." Mrs. Victoria Selkirk, a subdued version of her mother-in-law, spoke from the far end of the table. "If he had business with Lady Bisterne, then he had business with her and it's none of our business."

"Are you still free this afternoon?" Pierce asked Tristram.

Before he could assure Pierce he was, Mrs. Caroline Selkirk began to speak again.

"Catherine always was a wild one." The eldest lady scooped butter onto a bite of roll. "And the younger one is following in her footsteps. How they managed to produce such a quiet and steady son is beyond my comprehension. Paul Three works hard in the city every day." She fixed her gaze on Pierce. "Unlike some young men I know."

Pierce laughed, but the entrance of a footman with a bowl of steaming soup paused the dialogue. He set the bowl before Tristram. Aromas of leeks and creamy chicken stock reminded him he hadn't eaten for hours and had taken two walks in the cold. If he wasn't careful, he might gobble down the food like a barbarian.

"Paul VanDorn," Pierce said once the footman departed, "is dull."

"I think he's very nice." Georgette spoke to her empty plate.

"And handsome," her mother added.

"It's a handsome family." Pierce grinned.

Mrs. Selkirk the elder banged her cane on the floor like a gavel. "Handsome is as handsome does, and they haven't done handsomely yet."

"Perhaps," Mrs. Victoria Selkirk said, "but Lady Bisterne is a friend of Lord Tristram's, and we should watch what we say around him."

"She can't be friends to anyone after what she did to our George—"

"Grandmother, please." Georgette's hands flew to her cheeks, which were once again the color of the peonies in the gardens back at Cothbridge.

Tristram devoted himself to his soup and pretended not to notice.

After the pause for servants to deliver plates of fish and vegetables, Pierce began a discussion of when they should take the train to New York and what they should see there. That got them through the meal without more remarks about the VanDorn family. Instead Mrs.

Caroline Selkirk turned her ire on Pierce for not taking the train into the city every day to work with his father.

Pierce, losing his good humor for once, flashed his grandmother an annoyed glance. "I do go into the city every day and work. I even do so on many Saturdays. But right now, I have a visit from a friend I haven't seen in eight years and am taking a holiday."

They agreed to take their dessert in the drawing room, knowing well that the old lady never ate away from a table and would go to her room to nap after the meal. The younger Mrs. Selkirk murmured something about counting linens and left her children and Tristram alone.

"I apologize for Grandmother," Georgette said the instant her mother departed. "She never used to be so bitter."

"Making Grandmother so bitter may be the worst crime Catherine . . . er . . . Lady Bisterne committed." Pierce stretched his legs toward the fire. "Grandmother grew up the daughter of a Pennsylvania coal miner. She was pretty enough to marry the boss, who in turn ended up owning the mine. But she has never forgiven how Catherine kept our family from climbing even higher than invitations to Mrs. Astor's annual ball."

"If rumors are true," Georgette said in her honey-sweet voice, "Catherine saved me from a difficult life. Still . . ." She shook her head. "Enough of that. Would you like to see the Statue of Liberty?"

They decided to leave for New York the next day. Mrs. Victoria Selkirk elected to join them for some shopping, and Ambrose and Florian, coming in late in the afternoon, thought they would enjoy the tour as well. They stayed in the city for three days, residing in the Selkirks' brownstone overlooking Central Park.

New York wasn't London. Nonetheless, Tristram enjoyed the sights, the fine restaurants, and the entertainments and dancing with Georgette at an impromptu party at the Selkirks' house. The only flaw in the excursion was the discovery of a pearl-and-ruby pendant that matched the description and drawing of one of the Bisterne baubles, sold to a jeweler on Fifth Avenue.

"Surely she wouldn't be so foolish as to sell something in her own back garden," Florian said.

"She was scarcely in town long enough to do so," Ambrose pointed out.

But the proof, bright and cold, lay on Tristram's palm, and Catherine's words rang in his ears, dark and cold and full of pain.

"Sometimes I think," Tristram said, "I should marry Georgette Selkirk and forget trying to prove that Lady Bisterne is a thief."

Florian choked on his tea. "What about your father? What about your inheritance?"

"Neither would matter if I married an heiress." Spoken aloud, it all sounded too calculating. "And yet, perhaps the old lady Selkirk could set aside her bitterness if her granddaughter caught herself a title."

"Especially if you end up acceding to the marquisate," Ambrose drawled. "She'd like a marquess being higher ranked than an earl."

"Perhaps it's the kinder option." Tristram could spare the VanDorns humiliation or worse and acquire a lovely wife.

He began to contemplate the notion of marriage more than a little seriously on the way back to Tuxedo Park. He and Georgette shared a seat and conversed with the ease of long-standing friends. Sitting beside her didn't make him feel as though he might be spitted at any moment. After another month, if this camaraderie continued, he would probably be foolish not to make Georgette an offer.

At least that was his thinking until he reached Tuxedo Park.

When Tristram was dressing for dinner, one of the footmen knocked on the bedroom door. "You have several messages and some mail, sir. I mean—"

"'Sir' is quite all right." Tristram took the correspondences off the tray the footman held out to him. "'Lord' is merely courtesy and holds very little meaning."

He took the messages and letters to the room's desk and sorted through them. Missives from his father he set aside for later beneath two letters from former army friends to read at his leisure. He read the handwritten messages, notations from telephone calls. They were invitations to dinners, a shooting party, and a musical evening. The last message left him standing, lips compressed, until the dinner bell rang.

The caller was Sims the butler, on behalf of Mrs. VanDorn, and had come through a mere quarter hour before the Selkirk party returned from the city. She was terribly sorry to be calling so tardily, but would he be willing to even up her table at a dinner party the following evening? The husband of one of her guests had been called away at the last minute, and she didn't wish for his wife to have to cry off as well.

And there it was whipping through him, that frisson of energy he experienced near Lady Bisterne at the mere suggestion he might see her again. It was a good enough reason to refuse.

The pearl-and-ruby pendant tucked into his handkerchief drawer was more than enough reason to say yes.

Georgette awaiting his courtship downstairs was good enough reason to say no.

The notion of Catherine getting away with stealing because she was a mistreated wife was good enough reason to say yes.

He settled himself at the desk, drew out stationery and pen, and wrote a note accepting the invitation.

CHAPTER 6

"People always talk to their neighbors at table whether introduced or not. It would be a breach of etiquette not to!" Emily Price Post

"You did what, Mama?" Seated on a sofa in the drawing room, Catherine looked up from her needlework to stare at her parent with horror.

Estelle glanced up from the music score she was studying. "You could at least have invited Mr. Baston-Ward or Mr. Wolfe."

"And so I would have, had Lord Tristram declined." Mama stood at a refectory table at one end of the room, arranging flowers in a crystal bowl, chrysanthemums in shades of orange, gold, and yellow sent up fresh from the city. This one would grace the center of the table. Other smaller bowls already stood on tables throughout the public rooms.

If only she could wear her gold gown from Paris, Catherine lamented. It would show well with the color theme Mama had chosen for the dinner party décor. Instead, she would behave herself and wear a velvet gown so deep a purple it looked black away from direct lighting. Perhaps a little gold jewelry would set it off nicely. Just a little and, with Tristram coming, only pieces she owned before or since her time in England.

"I don't know why you two are objecting to his lordship," Mama said.

"He's not truly a lord, you know." Catherine had spent months learning how the English peerage worked. "He's still a commoner."

"Unless his sister-in-law produces a girl." Estelle made the comment without looking up from her scribbling on the musical score.

Catherine startled. "What do you mean? He has an older brother."

Estelle glanced up. "You didn't know? His brother died seven months ago."

Long enough for him to be out of mourning for a sibling.

"I didn't know." Catherine shook her head. "I left England a year ago August and had as little as possible to do with anyone from the English aristocracy as I could."

"You need to rid your heart of this bitterness, Catherine." Mama's dark eyes clouded with sadness. "I'm certain they aren't all like your husband."

Catherine grimaced. "Lord Tristram's older brother was."

"He'd been drinking heavily and fell from his horse," Estelle confirmed. "Mr. Wolfe told me to let me know now he's only third in line to the title if Lady, um—what is her name?"

"Her husband's courtesy title was Harriford."

In one of the two times she'd been able to go to London, Catherine had seen the lady in a dressmaker's shop. She was a pretty, petite blonde with a sweet-faced daughter in tow. She had been apologizing to a shop girl for how badly the young woman's employer had been treating her for some imagined slight to her ladyship, a genuine kindness from a lady who deserved better than the current—at the time—heir to the Marquess of Cothbridge.

"I hope for her sake," Catherine mused aloud, "she has a girl. That will free her to marry someone more of her choosing. But if she has a boy, she'll be stranded at Cothbridge and under the marquess's thumb."

"If she has a girl," Estelle pointed out, "Lord Tristram will inherit the title."

"Which is likely why he's here in America." Mama took a half-dozen steps back from her flower arrangement. "He's looking to find an American heiress."

"He doesn't need an heiress if he inherits," Catherine said. "The Wolfes are quite wealthy. Why would he need his own income?"

"Apparently," Estelle explained, "his father is so angry with him for resigning his army commission that he has cut him off unless he does something important."

Catherine's finger slipped, and she jabbed her embroidery needle into her finger.

"How romantic!" Mama returned to her flowers and began to tuck greenery around the edges of the bowl. "What sort of important thing must he do?"

Estelle furrowed her brow, wrote something on her score, then glanced up long enough to say, "I don't know. Mr. Wolfe wouldn't tell me, if he even knows."

Oh, he knew, as did Catherine. He needed to prove she was a thief and procure the rest of the jewelry she did not have. Probably even recover any money made selling the other pieces in Europe, which she didn't have because she had never obtained it. She couldn't avoid him if Mama had invited him to dinner and he had accepted. Of course he had accepted.

An absurd image flashed through her mind—Lord Tristram Wolfe slipping up the servants' steps to find her bedchamber and rifle through her jewel box.

"Could you not invite him and Mr. Baston-Ward to the party as well?" Estelle was asking.

"I'd have had to find two more single ladies in that event." Mama started to lift the heavy crystal bowl of flowers, then swept across the room to the bell. "Mr. Harold Padget already accepted my invitation, so when Mr. Rutlidge couldn't come, I had to scramble for another bachelor to make the table even."

Estelle heaved a sigh strong enough to have fanned the flames on the hearth had she sat closer to the fire. "I suppose Mr. Harriman is for me?"

Which meant Tristram would escort Catherine into dinner instead of her brother.

"He is quite unexceptionable as a suitor, Estelle." Mama directed her attention to the footman who had responded to her ring.

He carried the bowl out of the room. Mama followed, no doubt to supervise its placement on the table.

Estelle covered her eyes with her hand. "Mr. Harriman is nearly twice my age and doesn't know an A from an F. I've heard him try to sing in church."

Catherine examined her finger for blood. If this kept up, her fingers would resemble pin cushions. With no harm done this time, she resumed her embroidery. "And Lord Tristram doesn't like me."

"Ha." Estelle flashed Catherine a grin. "That's not how it looked in the music room the other day. He couldn't take his eyes off you."

"Probably afraid I'd steal his tie pin," Catherine muttered.

"What did you say?"

"Never mind." Catherine set her needlework into its basket and lifted the handle. "I'm going for a walk. Do you want to join me?"

Estelle glanced out the window at the pale blue sky free of clouds. "It looks cold, and I don't wish to risk chapping my hands. I'm going to go practice before Mama returns and finds something for me to do for this party. It is going to be so very dull if I have to entertain Mr. Harriman."

"Unless you attach yourself to the ladies planning the charity tea."

"It's a good notion." Estelle slipped through the narrow door leading from drawing to music room.

Catherine climbed to her room to fetch a hat and coat for a brisk walk along the lakeshore. She had grown fond of walking during her years in England. It got her away from the never-ending hammering and sawing and fumes from paints and varnishes as her money repaired the manor. Only the rainiest days held her inside, and she had kept up the practice once back in New York.

She set off down the path leading to the lake. Though the sun blazed in the sky, ice rimmed the lake. In no time, they would be able to ice-skate or toboggan. She gave a little hop of excitement at the prospect. Ice and snow were as foreign to Romney Marsh as she had been. Soon, perhaps, if she could make her peace with Georgette, Tuxedo Park would be home again. But Georgette hadn't responded to any of her notes. Between that and Lord Tristram determined to ruin her, she doubted anywhere could be home.

If Tuxedo Park could no longer be where she belonged, then where? Europe had been interesting and beautiful, but she did not belong there with her mediocre French and bad Italian. Perhaps she could go west and be plain Catherine VanDorn again.

Contemplations on belonging needed to wait. If she didn't head home, only a miracle would get her ready for the party on time. Preparing for the party meant more than donning an evening gown and appropriate jewelry.

She must work out how to manage Lord Tristram Wolfe.

∞

Tristram's mouth went dry at the sight of Lady Bisterne. In a purple gown that emphasized her long neck surrounded by a circlet of flat gold-and-enamel plaques, she looked like a queen. If Edwin Bisterne had married her only for her fortune, then he had been a bigger fool than Tristram believed.

And if the late earl had indeed married Catherine for her money, then perhaps he owed her those jewels.

Poised in the doorway to the VanDorn drawing room for half a minute longer than he should, Tristram watched Catherine ministering to the oldest of the guests. She tucked a pillow behind the back of an aged matron he already knew from experience was more than a little crotchety, then she glided across the floor, her velvet skirts swirling around her feet like a dark cloud, to move a fire screen to better reflect the heat toward an old man with twinkling eyes. A middle-aged gentleman caught her hand as she passed. Instead of giving him the setdown he deserved, she offered him a brilliant smile and said something that made him not only release her fingers but laugh while he let her go.

And Tristram's conscience bit deep. Believing her guilty of theft—especially once he realized she disliked her husband enough to want revenge—was easy when he wasn't with her. But this gracious and elegant lady could surely not so much as contemplate stealing her wedding ring, let alone an entire vault full of jewelry.

Yet she had kept her wedding ring and the rest.

Deciding he had been the fool this night for accepting the invitation, he entered the drawing room. Mr. VanDorn came toward him, one hand extended in greeting, the other holding a cup wafting steam.

"Hot cider after what was surely a cold ride over." Mr. VanDorn gave Tristram the cup.

"I walked." Tristram took the cup and wrapped his hands around it. "I enjoy walking, weather permitting."

"You sound like my daughter." Mr. VanDorn didn't say which one, but his gaze flicked across the room toward Catherine. "Which reminds me, she is your dinner partner."

Of course she was. Social precedent dictated the two of them would be seated either across from or next to one another. No doubt his hostess would be on the other side.

"Allow me to make a few introductions for you." VanDorn set his hand on Tristram's shoulder. Then he proceeded to make introductions to some people with names Tristram recognized because they occasionally made news in the English papers.

"Dinner's about to be announced," Mr. VanDorn said, "so I'll leave you with my eldest daughter."

The circuit of the room ended in front of Catherine and more windows offering a spectacular view of the lake beneath a full moon. She stood close enough to the window that her breath fogged the glass, blurring her reflection. His was perfectly clear beside hers. So was the image of her father walking away.

"Good evening, Lord Tristram." She raised one hand, on which sparkled an amethyst the size of a quail egg. The scent of springtime swirled around her, violets and lily of the valley.

Tristram's nostrils flared. He couldn't think of anything to say. He watched her reach toward the glass, half expecting her to write in the steam. Instead, she started to use the lace frill at the bottom of her sleeve.

"Allow me." He reached past her and wiped away the fog with his handkerchief.

She faced him. "Why did you come?"

"I can't ferret out your secrets if I don't ever see you."

"All you will learn is that I have no secrets." Indeed, her deep-blue eyes were wide and as guileless as a child's.

Too guileless.

He gave her his own limpid gaze. "We shall see. I—"

The dinner bell rang, and couples began to form.

Tristram offered her his arm. For a moment, she remained motionless as though she were about to refuse his offer. Then, as the last of the other couples left the drawing room, she laid her fingertips on his forearm. Just her fingertips. She may as well have pressed hard upon each of the nerves in his forearm. He needed all his self-control not to jerk away from a reaction that must be wholly wrong. He was pursuing her, not courting her.

He reached the dining room on feet that felt as though he wore overlarge Wellingtons rather than light evening shoes fitted for him. To his relief, she released his arm the instant they reached their places. A footman drew out her chair. She settled into it with fluid grace. As soon as Mr. VanDorn asked the blessing over the meal, Catherine turned to the gentleman on her right, leaving Tristram to his hostess through the soup course. She was practiced at polite dialogue, asking him questions about his family, then his work.

"Though I suppose you don't work, do you? Such a difference between England and America. Even the men in our best families work."

"Besides some charity work, I've been helping my father manage his land holdings since my brother's passing. That, ma'am, is a great deal of work."

"Oh, and how much land is that?" Her tone suggested it was no bigger than a farm.

He shrugged. "Twenty thousand acres."

She choked on her sip of soup.

"It's a respectable size." For no good reason, he wanted her to know his branch of the family had enough money so that he didn't need an heiress. "Nothing like what is possessed by those of you out in the west."

"But more civilized."

They had a rapport after that, this lady who was a fine image of what Catherine would look like in twenty years—poised and still beautiful with those fine bones.

Beautiful as long as Catherine didn't let anger over her husband's treatment of her etch lines of bitterness into her face instead of the smile marks Mrs. VanDorn's face bore. Catherine's mother was a happy woman who glowed whenever she mentioned the name of one of her children. Pure motherly pride he could shatter.

He felt like a hypocrite eating at her table.

When the salad course arrived and Mrs. VanDorn turned to the man on her left, Tristram switched his attention to Catherine. She looked at her plate. She stabbed a strip of lettuce and moved it from one side to the other, set her fork down, sipped water, then resumed the lettuce relocation process. Not once did she so much as take a bite or glance at him from the corner of her eye.

"Isn't not speaking to me unforgivably rude?" he finally asked.

"Isn't coming to the home of people whose daughter you've accused of theft unforgivably rude?"

He winced. "I could perhaps prove your innocence, too, you know."

"You could choose to believe me." She set down her fork and gave up on the pretense of eating.

"Please, let us converse like civilized beings." Beneath the edge of the tablecloth, he pressed his right hand over her left.

Her hand twitched, but she did not draw it away. "Talk about what? I'm rather out of practice with social repartee."

"Tell me about your favorite places on the Continent."

"The Alps?" She sounded uncertain, her words tentative. "We have magnificent mountains in this country, though I have never seen them, but the Alps were . . . well, who needs a cathedral for worship when one has places like that?"

"You prefer the mountains to Florence or Rome?"

"I do. Paintings are all well and good, but nature . . ." Her hesitation vanished the more she talked, and by the end of the meal, when Mrs. VanDorn rose to lead the ladies from the room, he had discovered many interests he and Catherine shared—land, quiet, and things of beauty like towering mountains and well-written books. She was pretty and intelligent, and she possessed a gift for witty observation.

Under other circumstances, he would have loved to spend more time in her company. He would love to spend more time in her company anyway.

For now, he was stranded in the dining room with a dozen men he barely knew. Tristram accepted a tiny glass of port and leaned back in his chair. Knowing too little of American politics to join in the discussion of President McKinley's reelection the day before, Tristram listened with partial concentration in the event someone addressed him directly. The rest of the time, he concentrated on how he should proceed with his investigation into Catherine and the jewels. By the time Mr. VanDorn suggested they join the ladies, Tristram had his answer.

CHAPTER 7

"The ideal partner is one who never criticizes or even seems to be aware of your mistakes, but on the contrary recognizes a good maneuver on your part, and gives you credit for it whether you win the hand or lose . . ." Emily Price Post

Tristram found Catherine dispensing coffee and tea from a low table at one end of the drawing room. Estelle carried the cups to ladies settled in groups around the chamber. When Tristram approached her, she slid a cup of tea toward him without looking higher than the middle button on his waistcoat.

"I don't care for tea." He glanced around for a chair light enough for him to move it closer to her. None was free, and the nearest seat was the other cushion of the settee on which she perched. "May I?" He didn't wait for an answer. Expecting it to be no, he settled beside her.

"You don't care whether anyone thinks you're paying special attention to me." She spoke in an undertone no one but he could hear.

"She speaks." He lowered his voice as well.

She lifted the coffeepot and started to pour.

"No more." Estelle approached the table. "Some people are leaving. I shall entertain the rest of the guests." She sailed off for the music room, her fingers moving at her sides as though she already played an instrument.

"Excellent. No interruptions." He half turned on the settee so he could see Catherine better.

With a number of remaining guests casting them speculative glances, she could stay as she was, stiff-backed, hands folded in her lap, giving him her profile; she could stand and leave; or she could angle herself so they could talk more directly. The first two choices would be unforgivably rude from a social perspective and would be subjects for gossip. The third option could suggest that he was courting her or, at the least, entering into a flirtation, also a possible subject for gossip.

She took so long to move he feared she would risk rudeness. Then, just as the strains of a violin began to drift from the music room and he considered bidding goodnight to save her embarrassment, she picked up the cup he had rejected and turned just enough to hand it to him.

"Drink your fill." She set the cup and saucer into his hands. "If I remember from when the Selkirks and I were inseparable, their cook makes terrible tea—by English standards."

"Nothing has changed." Although tea this late at night would keep him up for hours, he sipped it, inhaling the fragrance of bergamot and orange pekoe blended with Catherine's spring-flower scent, the latter as likely to keep him awake as the former. "I considered purchasing a spirit lamp and tea in the city so I could make my own in my room."

"I'd like to see the old lady's face if you had." She laughed.

He warmed to his toes. "A gross breach of etiquette?"

"Though you might get away with it as simple English eccentricity."

"Then I should have done so." He set the cup and saucer back on the table, wanting nothing but clear air between them. "Or I may come here whenever I need a cup of real tea."

Her folded hands turned into clenched fingers. "You don't wish to do that."

"Ah, but I do."

"Why?" She slid so close to the edge of her cushion he feared she would tumble to the flowered carpet.

He rested his arm on the back of the settee, too far from her shoulders for the gesture to be inappropriately intimate, but hinting to the others in the room that he intended this conversation to remain private in plain sight. "I intend to become one of your greatest admirers."

"You intend to what?" Everyone might have been able to hear her exclamation if the violin recital hadn't exploded into a lively gypsy melody.

He grinned. "I intend to become one of your greatest—"

"I heard you the first time." Voice lowered, she waved one hand in the air as though erasing a chalkboard. "I meant what do you think you're playing at with such a suggestion?"

"No game."

"Ha. Your being here at all is some kind of May game. Did the Baston-Ward family put you up to it? Did they . . . Did they . . ." She struggled for words or thoughts, then her eyes narrowed. "Did they send someone to sell the jewels in my wake to make me look guilty and extort funds from me?"

"A thought I hadn't considered." The violin dropped into something slow and dream-like, so he lowered his voice to a mere murmur. "With good reason. The jewels were missing when the new earl first opened the safe."

"And do you only have their word for it?"

"I have my father's word for it. Whereas with you, I only have your word for the truth. And since my father has nothing to gain and a great deal of money to lose by whatever game you are playing with the jewelry, I am taking his word over yours."

"Then do you hope for the opportunity to sneak into my room and search my jewel case if you come here enough?"

"I expect you're too good a player to keep them near your person." He brushed his fingertips across her velvet-clad shoulder, rose, and bowed. "I shall call on you as soon as my host's plans permit." He started to turn away.

"I won't be at home." He barely heard her above the lively Scottish tune coming from the violin. "Unless you're willing to perform a service for me in return."

Saying nothing about his suspicions and the evidence were quite enough of a favor, and if he could gain her cooperation without a struggle, he would do anything he could, even if it did incur his father's wrath.

"And what is that?" He drew out the question to convey his ambiguity.

She lifted her gaze to meet his, and her lake eyes looked as soft as her gown. "Arrange a meeting between Georgette Selkirk and me, and I will be happy to be at home when you call."

It was a foolish promise for him to make, that he could effect a reunion between Catherine and Georgette. Although he saw Georgette daily, he rarely spoke to her alone for more than a minute or two. Conversation was difficult over the net of a tennis court at the Tuxedo Park racket club during those warm days the Americans called Indian summer. He couldn't bring up such a personal topic during dinner or a party, though he was tempted in the middle of a waltz. Except in the middle of that waltz, he caught sight of Catherine across the room and wished he were spinning her around the dance floor.

He saw her in snatches, brief dialogues in the great hall clubhouse, on the verandah where she drank tea with local ladies in the warm autumn sun, or at the home of someone bold enough to invite both Selkirks and VanDorns. He never mentioned the jewels. She never mentioned Georgette, and he walked away feeling as though the exchanges held more value than hours spent in others' company. Each exchange showed him a lady who loved her family, found beauty even in a rainy day, and wanted to do something useful with her life. After learning this last bit of information, he planned to call on her to talk about his mission so she would understand why finding the jewels for his father was so important to him, when the Selkirks decided to return to the city. Reluctantly, Florian, Ambrose, and Tristram went along, as they had little choice with their host and the female family members going.

"I'll do some hunting through the jewelry and pawn shops." Ambrose gave Tristram a pointed glare. "Since you seem to have given up the hunt, perhaps your father will give me a reward if I prove the woman took the jewels and get the rest back."

"Not to mention the money she got for the ones she sold." The corners of Florian's lips drooped. "Though I admit I'm finding it harder and harder to believe she's guilty. She's so quiet and kind."

"And Estelle's sister." Ambrose cuffed him on the shoulder.

"No, seriously. In spite of how we've made this horrible accusation against her," Florian said, "she still treats us with all that's gracious."

As she treated Tristram.

"Don't trust her," Ambrose snapped. "Remember how she schemed to get Bisterne away from Miss Selkirk."

Tristram's upper lip curled. "I doubt he needed much persuasion once he learned the size of her dowry outshone Miss Selkirk's."

"And she's nearly as pretty as her sister." Florian cast an oblique glance at Tristram. "Don't you think, Tris?"

"Prettier." The word slipped out before he could stop himself.

Both his companions stared at him.

"No wonder you've stopped trying to get the jewelry back," Ambrose murmured. "You're besotted with her."

"You'd better tell the beauteous Georgette," Florian added. "She has her cap firmly set in your direction."

"Don't be absurd." Tristram shrugged off their remarks with more nonchalance than he felt. "We, all of us, scarcely know one another."

But they teased him mercilessly until the third day in the city, when Georgette suggested he take a walk with her in Central Park.

Ambrose and Florian had gone to witness some low form of entertainment in the area known as the Bowery. Pierce had accompanied his mother and grandmother to visit their dressmaker, but Georgette stayed behind.

"It's too fine a day to stay indoors getting poked and prodded and stuck full of pins." Georgette gave Tristram a pointed glance. "I can persuade you to take me to the park for a brisk walk, can I not?"

"You may." Tristram, too, welcomed a long, fast walk through the park.

Indeed, now that he was truly alone with Georgette, other than the scores of strangers passing them in both directions, he didn't know how to start a conversation with her.

Georgette broke the silence. "I never realized you were so shy. You never seem at a loss when Pierce is with us."

Tristram's ears heated despite the biting wind blowing from the west. "I haven't spent a great deal of time with single females between school, university, and then the army. Not young and pretty ladies, that is."

"You place me in that category?" She tilted her head to peek up at him from beneath the wide brim of her hat. A little smile played about her lips.

"I should think your mirror tells you the truth of that every day."

Georgette heaved a sigh audible above the cries of children playing a game of tag beside the path. "You sound like my grandmother when I was a green girl. Now she tells me to look in my mirror and see how I'm aging."

"Nary a wrinkle I can find." He made a show of inspecting her face for telltale signs of aging.

"I see many. Perhaps you need spectacles." She laughed up at him.

"Perhaps your mirror is losing its silvering."

Her blue eyes sparkling, tendrils of blonde hair blowing around the perfect oval of her face, she was more than pretty, with her ready smile and delicate features. But looking into her crystal-blue eyes didn't coil his insides like a spring ready to snap; therefore, he shouldn't flirt with her. He shouldn't give her any reason to hope for anything but friendship from him.

"And I've seen how the men wish to dance with you," he added.

"Men I've known all my life like I know Pierce. So boring. Well, not boring precisely, but too familiar or unavailable."

Tristram arched one brow. "Do you mean someone in particular?"

"It wouldn't matter if I did." She wrinkled her nose as though the sharp scent of fallen and dried leaves carpeting path and grass displeased her. "I'm considering going to Europe to find some variety. Of course, having variety come to us has helped my ennui a great deal." She pressed her fingers into his arm.

"We appreciate the hospitality of your family." Tristram hesitated, then plunged. "Everyone in Tuxedo Park has been cordial and welcoming. I quite enjoyed many of the entertainments, including the one at the VanDorns'."

"Of course you did." The corners of her mouth drooped. "Mrs. VanDorn sets a fine table, and none of them is anything but intelligent and kind."

"Including Lady Bisterne?" The instant he spoke the title Georgette had lost, he regretted it, but he could scarcely call her Catherine aloud.

Georgette paused on the path and gazed out across a pond, her back half toward him. "Catherine has well paid for her actions of five years ago, I understand."

"She would like to speak with you. She asked me if I would effect a meeting."

She spun to face him. "Why?"

"I believe she feels badly—"

Her shoulders tensed. "No, no, why did she ask you to play envoy?"

"Because I was available to ask."

The tension left her, and she smiled. "In that event, I will call on her when we return."

"I will be happy to escort—"

"No." One sharp word, then she grasped his arm and started walking. "My family won't approve of me going there with you."

Because they wanted a match between him and their daughter. Yet Georgette was no more interested in anything beyond friendship than he was. That should leave him free to spend time with Catherine. Yet the Selkirks did not like the VanDorns, and if he began to hang about with Catherine instead of Georgette, he might no longer be welcome in the Selkirk home. Without their sponsorship, he could not remain in Tuxedo Park, he would be unable to pursue the jewel thief, and he would damage his chances of reconciliation with his father.

Unless he and Georgette pretended to be courting. His heart rebelled at the notion of being deceptive, but perhaps the end justified a little harmless misdirection.

Tristram halted, his hand on her arm. "Miss Selkirk, would your interests be better served if your family thought you and I had the beginnings of an understanding?"

"An understanding?" She reared back as though he had struck her. "Lord Tristram, please, no. You must not."

"I am not—or I expect it to lead to nothing."

"Ah." Her face lit with laughter. "A little game to throw Grandmother off the scent. That just might work—better than you know." Her face lost its brightness as she gazed along the path the way they had come. "It will keep other gentlemen from courting me."

Tristram followed her gaze and saw a young man feeding bread to the pigeons beside the pond. Tristram did not recognize him until the train ride back to Tuxedo Park when he saw the same gentleman with an older version of himself.

So Georgette bore a *tendre* for Paul VanDorn III.

∽

What nonsense Catherine had spoken when she declared she would be happy to be at home the next time Lord Tristram Wolfe called. Nothing about the man made her happy. On the contrary, being near him left her restless and dissatisfied with what—the brevity of their surprisingly delightful dialogues? Angry with the fact he didn't call for another week and a half? That lengthy lack of contact should make her happy.

Until the past few days, Florian and Ambrose had visited far more often than was proper. Since they spent all that time in the music room with Estelle, the sessions seemed harmless enough. What was not harmless was how often Estelle danced with Florian at two entertainments. But she laughed off Catherine's concerns and lamented the three of them had nowhere to perform the pieces they had been working on.

"Music should not be hidden behind closed doors," Estelle declared.

"But, child," Mama protested, "you are a debutante. You can't perform in public."

"I did at the ball and—"

"Wait." Catherine lifted her hand from the list of Tuxedo Club residents she was going over for invitations to the charity tea the week after Thanksgiving Day. "I don't see why they can't entertain the guests at the tea. We can spend more money on gifts for the children if we don't have to pay professional entertainers to provide the music."

"I don't know." Mama frowned.

Estelle leaped to her feet and hugged Catherine. "Thank you. Thank you. Are you inviting Lord Tristram? It would seem appropriate, if his friends are the entertainment."

"I'll be sending an invitation to the Selkirks, of course. All the residents will be receiving one." She bent her head over her list. "Not that I expect anyone from there to attend."

Estelle poked Catherine's arm. "I should think Lord Tristram would come. The two of you looked rather friendly at our dinner party."

"And he and Georgette looked rather cozy at Mrs. Vanderleyden's soirée." Catherine excused away the squeezing of her middle at this memory with her regret that she and Georgette had been so close yet hadn't so much as made eye contact.

Five years ago, they would have dragged one another off to discuss their plans for the evening before facing the crowd—the young men—together.

"He's obligated to play the gallant to the sister of his host," Mama pointed out. "Though you would think he might have managed a call if only to leave his card in thanks for our invitation to the dinner party. But if he comes to the tea, you may reacquaint yourselves."

"Not that Catherine wants another Englishman for a husband."

Catherine scowled at her sister. "Not that Catherine wants another husband. I am making myself quite content helping Mama plan this tea. And Mrs. Rutherford has asked me to help her plan her annual Christmas charity ball in the city. She hasn't been well and thinks because I lived in Europe for five years I should know all that is fashionable and refined." She laughed.

Mama's face lit. "Catherine, that is wonderful. What an honor."

"Even if she is quite mistaken about your life overseas." Estelle executed a pirouette and ended up at the door to the music room. "I must see what music will be suitable for the tea. Something proper for the month of Christmas, yes? May I send a note around to Fl—Mr. Baston-Ward and Mr. Wolfe?"

"I shall do so on your behalf." Mama rose from the sofa where she had been working at a bit of embroidery. "Catherine, may I use the desk?"

"I'll go into the library." Catherine gathered up her lists for the tea and charity ball and moved next door.

Scents of leather from the hundreds of books lining the shelves and the heavy, masculine furniture contrasted with the sweet orange aroma from the oil rubbed into the desk. It gleamed beneath sunlight streaming through the windows and providing warmth to the room, despite the frigid outside temperature.

The sun wouldn't last for long. Clouds piling up in the north predicted sleet or snow before evening. Catherine hoped it would arrive late enough that Papa and Paul Three didn't get stranded in the city, but early enough that that night's entertainment would be canceled.

It was a dance strictly for young people, and she had been designated as Estelle's chaperone. She wanted something to do with her life, but acting like she was forty-four rather than twenty-four was unacceptable. Whether she thought she wanted to or not, Estelle would marry within a year or two, and then what would Catherine do? Her parents were too young to need her to stay with them. And she was too used to running her own household to be happy living with Mama's management.

For now, she was happy to plan the two charity events. The invitations to the tea needed to go out within the next day or two, and decisions needed to be made there. Should she send Lord Tristram a separate invitation so he could come even if the Selkirks refused? Judging from Georgette's and Pierce's behavior at the Rutlidge soirée the previous week, they would refuse. Tristram was harder to predict. His courtship of Georgette was obvious.

They had danced together twice at the Vanderleydens' and not with anyone else. The rest of the time, they remained on the side of the drawing room with Pierce. The three of them talked and laughed together like old friends. Though they had enjoyed brief conversations over the preceding weeks, Tristram hadn't so much as tried to catch Catherine's eye. She concluded that he had been unable to persuade Georgette to mend the past or, at the least, make a truce between the families.

Her heart heavy, Catherine bent to the task of addressing envelopes for the tea. Into each one would go an invitation and return card. *Mrs. Paul VanDorn II and Lady Catherine Bisterne invite you . . .*

A discreet notation in the bottom corner of the return card indicated the minimum donation the attendee was to include with the *Répondez, s'il vous plaît.*

As she wrote, the muted strains of Estelle's banjo penetrated through the wall of books, but not the smooth, liquid way in which she played. This musician was inexpert with the instrument. She must be teaching someone. Florian and Ambrose must have called.

She'd gotten so used to the men coming over to play music in the afternoons, she paid them little attention. She didn't approve, but if Mama chose to not put a stop to the visits, Catherine could do nothing about it. She had, after all, recommended Mama not interfere and let the novelty of the Englishmen run its course.

The last invitation addressed and sealed, she rose and stretched. The sun had vanished and a chill penetrated the chamber.

So did a silence.

Catherine tilted her head and listened. Not a sound reached the library save for the wind sighing through the trees.

Uneasiness clamping her middle, she left the room and slipped into the drawing room next door. Mama and her needlework had gone. The music room door stood open, and Catherine crossed to stand in the doorway.

Florian perched on the piano stool. Estelle crouched before him. One of his hands held the banjo. The other curled around Estelle's fingers as they gazed into one another's eyes.

A hundred words of remonstrance rose in Catherine's throat. None emerged. A lump lodged in their way, the bitter ache of longing for someone to look at her with adoration, as Florian gazed at Estelle. Edwin had never once looked at Catherine like that.

As quietly as she could, Catherine took a step back and turned away. Her skirt rustled, but not loudly enough to interrupt the young people. She would find Mama and tell her about the couple.

She found Mama in the housekeeper's room discussing arrangements for the tea. Perhaps Catherine's face showed something, for the housekeeper rose with some excuse about ensuring they didn't need any provisions from the village before the storm hit in full, and left Catherine and Mama alone.

"I'm afraid Florian and Estelle are developing an affection for one another," Catherine blurted.

"I know." Mama toyed with her fountain pen. "It's not the sort of match we would like for her, but if it dispels this notion of becoming a musician, it makes your father and me happy. He seems to be a nice young man."

"He is. Or at least I never heard of him engaging in riotous living, and he's been coming to church, but he has no prospects. He's too much of a gentleman to work."

"Neither, my dear, did your husband, yet you saw fit to elope with him." Though the rebuke was subtle, it stung.

Rubbing the back of her neck, Catherine turned away. "I thought a title and land were enough. Now that I know so much more is necessary for a husband, I doubt I'll ever find another one."

"You will if the right gentleman comes along." Mama's voice was gentle. "Lord Tristram—"

"Has no interest in me." Catherine cut Mama off before she could suggest he was a potential mate. "And he's not only English, he's potentially heir to a title. Once for that was quite enough. I will find a dear American husband or none at all. Now, I shall go chaperone those two before hand-holding leads to something inappropriate."

She reached the corridor just as Florian prepared to leave. Estelle, rather than a footman, was handing him his hat and gloves.

He started to clasp Estelle's fingers, then saw Catherine and drew back. "Lady Bisterne, how do you do?"

"Fine, thank you. And you? Ambrose?"

"He's in the city with the Selkirks." Florian grinned. "Seems he met some minor heiress there he's thinking of courting. But we got bored squiring the ladies around to all their shopping, so Tris and Pierce and I came back here last evening."

No wonder she hadn't seen any of them, even from a distance, for several days. Perhaps now Tristram would call. She wished she could think of a message for Florian to give Tristram, but nothing came to her, so she said good-bye and returned to the library.

The floor-to-ceiling windows framed the first flakes of snow beginning to fall. Over the next two hours, while she curled up in a chair before the fire and read, the storm turned into the first significant snowfall of the season, with a white curtain so thick it blocked the view of the lake. Papa called to say he and Paul Three would stay at their club in the city. As night fell, the wind rose, howling around corners and rattling the windows. Estelle played the piano with thunderous chords to match the blizzard, and Mama went to bed early, complaining of drafts.

Catherine returned to the library alone, where she alternated sitting and pacing, trying to shake off the sense that the snow piled atop her like rocks. "I do not like this." She spoke aloud for the sound of a human voice. "Being here alone like this is unacceptable."

Once Estelle went to bed, the emptiness grew as bad as being at Bisterne—a house full of servants and her heart aching with loneliness. Unable to face the emptiness of her bedroom, she remained in the library reading until the wind died down and that peculiar hush of thick snowfall blanketed the world.

And she could bear the stillness no longer.

As quietly as she could, she raced up the steps to the third floor and the cedar-lined room in which they kept winter garments. From a corner, she unearthed her old fur-lined boots and muff never necessary during her marriage in Kent's milder climate. After slipping downstairs again, she donned the boots and bundled up in hat, scarf, and warm coat. Then she let herself outside through one of the library's French doors.

All her life she had adored being the first person to leave footprints in pristine snow. She might even toss off her veneer of staid widow and create a snow angel for the household to see in the morning and wonder over.

Laughing softly, she stepped off the verandah toward the edge of the lake.

Where hers were not to be the first footprints to mar the snow's perfection. By the light of a clearing sky full of stars, she caught sight of deep impressions in the white carpet, impressions twice the size of hers.

Her heart sank at the idea that a man had intruded upon her private moments of freedom. Getting inside the fence around Tuxedo Park wasn't easy, but it could be done. Most visitors were perfectly all right, but a woman alone at night must be careful.

She started to turn back to the house, but from the corner of her eye, she noticed that the footprints stopped in the vague direction of the walk from Lake House to shoreline. The deep impressions in the snow ended, and where they ceased, the body of a man lay crumpled against the trunk of a spruce.

CHAPTER 8

"The well-bred maid instinctively makes little of a guest's accident, and is as considerate as the hostess herself. Employees instinctively adopt the attitude of their employer." Emily Price Post

Though bright, the stars weren't clear enough for Catherine to distinguish the identity of the fallen man. Whether village worker, park resident, or someone's servant, he needed help and quickly. She first stooped to check his pulse. Finding one, she pulled off her coat and tossed it over him, then she raced for the house as quickly as six inches of snow allowed.

Every room was dark save for the library and her own chamber. She didn't feel comfortable going into the servants' quarters, but Sapphire would be in Catherine's chamber waiting to help her undress. She headed there, taking the steps two at a time, and flung open the door.

"Sapphire, we need two footmen and perhaps the housekeeper. Hot water. Perhaps bandages."

"Indeed, m'lady?" Sapphire set aside her knitting and rose from her seat by the fire. "Who is injured?"

"I don't know. I found him in the snow just now."

"The snow, m'lady?" Sapphire arched her finely plucked brows. "We will need a room made up for him then. Servants quarters or guest room?"

Catherine pressed a hand to her racing heart. "I won't know until we get him into the light."

"Then we had best do so quickly. Who knows how long he's been in the cold." With an easy stride that seemed slow but ate up a great deal of ground with each step, Sapphire headed for the back steps.

Catherine grabbed a cashmere shawl from a drawer and raced back into the snow. The man still lay there in a heap like a discarded ragdoll. His pulse still beat in his neck, but it was slow, and his skin felt barely warmer than the snow around him. With no idea what to do until the footmen arrived to carry the man to the house, she rubbed his cheeks with the fur muff warmed from her hands. She heard him groan once. Mostly she heard her own ragged breathing and her plea for his well-being, whoever he was.

Sapphire arrived and rested a hand on Catherine's shoulder. "We're here, m'lady. Let us take him in through the library so we can assess his condition and station."

"No, he needs to get warm swiftly. Take him straight to a guest room."

The footman looked at her askance, but Sapphire merely nodded and led the way through the house and up to the second floor, where a maid was building a fire on the hearth.

"Sapphire," Catherine said, "do you think of everything?"

"It's my duty, m'lady. I guessed you would want the man here regardless of his station. I have also sent for Dr. Rushmore."

"Of course you thought to do so." Catherine stepped out of the doorway so the footmen could lay their burden on the bed.

Light from a bedside lamp fell on the injured man's face. Catherine grasped the back of a nearby chair for support, a gasp escaping her lips. "Lord Tristram."

For a moment, the gold-tipped lashes swept upward, revealing eyes that looked less vibrant a green in his ashen face. "You look like an angel." He smiled, then his eyes closed again.

Suddenly too warm in her white cashmere shawl, Catherine backed out the doorway. "We will leave you men to remove his wet garments and make him comfortable." She turned on her heel and fled downstairs to wait for the doctor, to call Florian and Pierce, to forget he had called her an angel.

It meant nothing. He knew her as anything but something pure and good. He wanted to prove her even worse than a mere selfish creature. Now he might have plenty of opportunity to investigate if she weren't careful. If someone had been wily enough to plant the jewels in shops along her route through Europe, she wouldn't put it past the real thief to sneak into her house and place one of the stolen pieces in her dressing table or elsewhere. Given half a chance, she would have him moved back to the Selkirks' immediately.

But he couldn't be moved. Dr. Rushmore confirmed that prognosis to Catherine, Mama, and Estelle as they sat in the conservatory an hour later. "Slight concussion. Looks like he slipped in the snow and hit his head on that tree."

And did he say what he was doing there? She couldn't ask the doctor that.

"What was he doing on our lawn?" Mama carried no inhibitions about speaking with the young doctor.

He shook his head. "Out for a walk. Seems he's rarely seen this much snow in his life."

"He should stay until February." Estelle rubbed her arms. "He'll have more snow than he wants to."

"I still don't understand why he'd be all the way here." Mama sighed. "Young people these days. They make me feel old."

"Yes, Mama, you are positively ancient." Catherine kissed Mama's still-smooth cheek, then turned her attention to Dr. Rushmore. "What shall we do for him?"

"He needs rest, mostly. Keep him warm and look for signs of fever. Call me if he seems overly restless or flushed. I'll return tomorrow."

Mama rose. "I'll see you out, Doctor, then have the footmen take turns watching over him." She and Rushmore left the room.

Estelle faced Catherine and winked. "A rendezvous gone bad?"

"Not anything of the kind," Catherine snapped.

Estelle laughed. "You just happened to find him in the snow? Isn't that too much of a coincidence?"

"It is, but we had no arrangement. I do, however, believe he must have been coming to see me. Otherwise, he would have stayed with the road or the shore."

"Curious." Estelle yawned. "We shall have to wait for the morning to find out."

But Catherine knew she couldn't sleep until she had some kind of an answer. If Tristram was at all up to talking, she intended to speak to him.

With Mama and Estelle back in their rooms, she told the footman on duty to wait in the corridor for a minute with the door open, then bent over Tristram. "You're not sleeping."

"No, but you shouldn't be in here." His voice rose barely above a whisper.

"My mother is right across the hall, and there's a footman who can see me if not hear me talking this low, so bear with me for a moment, please."

"Just one?" The ghost of a smile tipped up the corners of his mouth. "Not several?"

A tremor ran through her at his words, and she responded in a sharp tone. "Stop flirting with me. I just need to know what you were doing on our lawn at half past nine o'clock at night."

"Coming to see you."

"Why?"

He started to shake his head, twisted up his face in pain, and raised his hands to press his palms against his temples. "Our bargain. Miss Selkirk."

"Is that all?" Disappointment leadened her stomach. "It could have waited until morning."

"No. You sent for me."

"I did not. I never would have."

"Of course you did. Glad of the excuse to call."

"But—we'll talk tomorrow when you're rested." She started to step back.

He caught hold of her hand. "Wait." With surprising strength, he drew her closer. "Wait. Must tell you."

"Tomorrow."

"No, please." His grip tightened. Strong, warm, tingling with current. "You know perfectly well." He took a deep breath. "I didn't fall and hit my head." He opened his eyes wide and held her gaze. "Someone hit me."

∞

Catherine's hand jerked in his, but she didn't let go. She stared at him with her eyes even larger than normal, and her face paled. "You must be mistaken."

He started to shake his head, but remembered how much doing so hurt and chose to smile instead. "Not mistaken. I have been hit in the head before." He touched his cowlick.

"But no one else was out in that weather."

"We were."

"Yes, but we're . . ." She looked away, and her cheeks turned the color of a ripe strawberry.

"Different from other people?"

Two of a kind. Rebellious. Too much alike in being disillusioned with the paths laid out for them.

Therein lay the words he could not say to her, the true reason why, the instant the snow ceased, he had welcomed the message telling him to call as soon as he could and headed down the hill to Lake House. Freed from the Selkirks' persistent round of activities in the city, where he and Georgette pretended to be growing in their regard for one another, he longed for a quiet verbal sparring match with the Dowager Countess of Bisterne.

He received a far different reception than he anticipated.

And he was a fool.

She drew her hand from his, and her mouth tightened. "I'm not different from other people. I follow the rules now."

He laughed and raised his hand, but couldn't reach her cheek. "You wouldn't be here if that were true."

"I was looking in on you to see if you need anything, is all." She took a step back. "Do you wish me to call the police? They're right outside the gate."

"I don't know. Let me rest."

Let him get his thoughts in order.

"I have no enemies of which I am aware." He glanced at her from the corner of his eye. "Except for you."

"However you got that blow on your head, my lord, it seems to have scrambled your wits." She half turned away. "Tell the footman if you need anything." Without bidding him goodnight, she left the room.

Tristram watched her go and laughed to himself. She might think she was following the rules. She might even follow them on the outside, but inside, she harbored a rebellious heart, a spirit that didn't agree with society's strictures that insisted ladies do nothing of much good. Wearing that purplish gown to the annual ball told him that the instant he set eyes on her.

"I know more about you than you think, my lady."

She hadn't spent the four years of imprisonment at Bisterne doing nothing but complaining about her miserable life and choosing wallpaper for bedrooms. At least once a month, she had visited every family dependent on the estate. If they needed anything, she saw that they received it, paying for it from her own money.

Another motivation for taking the jewels, for wanting to stop him from proving her guilt? Perhaps when the earl died, leaving her no right to remain in the house her money had restored, she thought the family owed her something.

Or perhaps she was not guilty.

The conflicting messages in his head made his bruised brain hurt more. He longed for sleep. The pain kept him awake. The picture of Catherine in her plain gray suit, so proper, so prim, yet her standing beside him holding his hand made him restless.

He wished Florian or Ambrose were there so he could talk to them. Even if they continued to vilify her, he would have welcomed the sound of her name. Catherine, the name of so many queens throughout history. Plain and simple, yet regal.

Despite her gray garb, nothing about Catherine was plain or simple. Nothing about his feelings for her was plain or simple. He adored her as much as he distrusted her. Yet now he had entered into bargains with Georgette, with his father, with himself, and he could break none of them if he wanted a future beyond tutoring ungrateful boys or sponging off his friends.

"I want peace, not this constant turmoil."

"Sir, um, my lord?" The footman spoke from his chair across the room.

"Never mind. Thinking aloud."

"All right. I'm here if you need anything." The young man settled back in the soft chair.

Tristram again tried to sleep. He tried to think of Georgette rather than Catherine, of making his false courtship of Georgette real since Catherine was out of the question for a lifelong mate. He tried to think of other ways the jewels could have gone missing. He tried to think of who might have bashed him on the head. And he failed at all of it.

Morning came before sleep claimed him and vanished far too soon with the arrival of Florian.

"What were you thinking, old man?" Florian drew the footman's abandoned chair closer to the bed and lounged against the winged back. "Wandering about in the dark and snow?"

"Walking about in the snow. It was a beautiful night."

"And what a convenient way to get into the lioness's den. Shall I nip down the hall and search her room?"

"While paying court to her sister? No."

Florian heaved an exaggerated sigh. "That's the rub of it, isn't it? She'll never have me if she finds out I've been helping you prove her sister is a jewel thief."

"I suppose there's an alternative." Tristram sat propped against pillows with a breakfast tray laid across his lap. Tea and buttered toast were all he could manage, but both eased his headache. He poured more tea from a blue china pot. "Such as prove she *isn't* a thief."

"What?" Florian shot upright. "What nonsense is this?"

"Probably just that—nonsense." Which turned the tea to acid and the toast to lead in his stomach.

"You can't possibly think she's innocent, can you?"

"I don't know what to think, but I'm no good lying here."

"I suppose you can't even talk to her."

Tristram said nothing of the midnight visit or his certainty that someone had struck him from behind. He discussed only the mundane with Florian, how he wanted the fresh air, how kind the VanDorn household had been to him, the logistics of him staying there.

"I need to get back to the Selkirks'."

"Dr. Rushmore says not to move you for at least two days in this weather." Florian yawned and stretched. "Gives me an excellent excuse to come by and stay for hours."

"And spend your time with your young lady rather than your ailing friend." Tristram mock scowled.

"She appreciates my company. You, I think, prefer someone else's. Pierce will be here shortly. Georgette is still in the city, if you care—which you do not."

"Then whose company other than lovely Miss Selkirk's could I possibly want?"

Florian laughed and departed.

Pierce came unaccompanied an hour later. His face was tight when the footman showed him into the sickroom, but it relaxed once he was alone with Tristram.

"Managed not to see any of the VanDorn ladies, have you?" Pierce asked.

"Not today."

Tristram heard her, though, her clear voice outside his door, the words indistinct, the tone of enquiry clear. If he could stand without the entire world spinning around him, he could walk across the carpet and catch every word, learn if she was talking about him or not.

"She won't come in here," Tristram added.

Pierce glanced around the room. "I didn't think I'd ever find myself in this house again."

"Which makes no sense. Don't you think you all should put this feud in the past? Ca—Lady Bisterne did something stupid, but it's over with."

"It won't be done with until Georgie marries." Pierce's long, narrow face grew even longer. "Her continued spinsterhood is a constant reminder that her fiancé was stolen out from under her nose by a member of this household. I am so happy you two seem to be forming an affection for one another. She is a great girl."

"She is."

The utter truth, but her heart was no more turned in his direction than his was in hers. If he had to guess, he would say the son of this very household held Georgette's interest.

Tristram crumbled a piece of toast. "I'll leave as soon as I can. Meanwhile, you needn't return."

"Oh no, I need to keep an eye on Georgie's interests." Pierce laughed as though intending to make a joke, but no mirth rang through.

Catherine might be a thief, Tristram wanted to say by way of reassurance. *Whatever her reasons.*

"I would like to see the feud end for all your sakes," he said instead. "Carrying on the animosity hurts you all more than it hurts Lady Bisterne."

"You always were a benevolent fellow." Pierce rose and opened a leather case he had brought with him. "Brought you some books you had in your room." He laid the volumes on a bedside table easy to Tristram's hand. "And a chessboard, if you're not too concussed to play."

"You want to take advantage of me to finally win a game."

Pierce snorted. "It would be a fine change. But first I want you to tell me what you were doing out and about in the snow. And here, of all places."

Tristram shrugged, winced, and laid his head back far enough that he looked at the crown molding on the wall. "I like the snow, especially when it's fresh like that. As for here? Will you believe coincidence?"

"No. And neither will Georgette." Pierce removed the dishes from the breakfast tray and began to set up the chessboard upon it as though it were a game table. "You paid a late call on Catherine the instant you could get away from us. I'd like to say asking you why is none of my business, but since my sister has decided she would like to be Lady—er—"

"Tristram. Odd to you Americans, I'm sure."

"Rather. But Georgie doesn't care how odd. It's a title, and there's your father's title."

"Which I may not inherit."

"You'll still have the other title. You take white this time."

They began to play, concentrating on their next several moves ahead rather than beautiful young spinsters seeking minor aristocracy for a spouse. Despite the dismissal of ladies as a topic, he played badly and lost the first game far too quickly.

"You looked tired." Pierce packed up the set. "Mrs. VanDorn has told me by way of the butler that I may come any time I like, so I'll leave you to rest and return later." He went to the door but paused. "I'm not mentioning this incident to Georgette. She'll be on the next train running from the city, and I don't think you want that right now."

"Not now."

Pierce left. Tristram rested and woke with a dull throb in his head instead of the crippling pain of earlier. Sometime while he slept, a footman had appeared. He sprang up the moment Tristram opened his eyes and offered to fetch shaving water and fresh clothes.

"The ladies would like to see you, my lord. Can you walk as far as the conservatory?"

"I can."

It took him several minutes longer than the walk of forty feet should have, with vertigo mixed with reluctance guiding him forward. The view of snow-clad lawn and trees and a lake glazed with ice made the effort worth the journey.

So did the appearance of Catherine in the doorway. She wore a dark blue dress trimmed in white lace around the high neck and puffy sleeves, and she carried a tray from which wafted the scent of chocolate. "My favorite snowy-day drink." She set the tray on the table. "Estelle will be here in a few minutes. She and Florian have some notion that you need soothing music to heal your head. But I asked her to wait so I could talk to you about what you said last night." She hesitated a moment, then sat on the sofa cushion beside him. "If you don't mind."

She appeared so domestic, so calm, he wanted to shove the distressing notion of her being a vengeful thief out of his head once and for all.

"I do not." On the contrary, he liked having her near more than he should. He twisted to face her. "I haven't changed my mind about what I told you. Someone did strike me from behind."

"But who and why? And why have you told me and no one else?"

"How do you know I've told no one else?"

"Pierce Selkirk would have had the police here, thinking he could blame us for it. Likely so would Florian."

"Which is why I didn't tell either of them."

"Again, why?"

He looked into her beautiful eyes and the answer caught in his throat, choking him. He swallowed and shook his head.

"Shall I pour some chocolate for you?" She reached for the tall silver chocolate pot.

"No, thank you. I feel badly enough accepting your hospitality under the circumstances."

"I think we are to extend hospitality to the needy regardless of circumstances. Love our enemies and all." She forced a laugh. "Not that you're my enemy, because you haven't yet worked out I'm not a jewel thief."

"That's the problem at stake, though, my lady. I haven't worked that out, and worse . . ." His eyes felt scorched.

"What can be worse than being accused of a crime you didn't commit?"

"Being accused of two crimes you may or may not have committed."

"Two crimes. What—?" She broke off the query with a gasp and sprang to her feet. "Are you suggesting that I am the one who struck you on the head?"

CHAPTER 9

"Since it is not likely that any one would go around the world being deliberately offensive to others, it may be taken for granted that obnoxious behavior is either the fault of thoughtlessness or ignorance—and for the former there is no excuse." Emily Price Post

Tristram looked her in the face, then turned away. "I considered it a possibility."

"You considered it? You thought even for a moment that I am capable of . . . of . . ." Catherine slid to her knees beside the sofa and gripped the coffee table. A lifetime of training kept her back straight when she wanted to bow forward under the weight upon her shoulders. "If you weren't too injured to be traveling on these roads, I'd tell you to leave."

"And I would rather not abuse your hospitality." He sounded so sad, she levered herself back onto the sofa and faced him. He gazed down at his hands clasping his knees. "I have been wrestling with this for hours. To take your kindness and then think something so heinous is unconscionable. I had to say something to you."

"You've said something to me." Unable to remain near him any longer for fear he would see the tears pooling in her eyes, she shot to her feet and stalked across the room to where she could see the tree that had broken his fall. No footprints remained. Snow had drifted into the impressions, and now melt from the sun had glazed over the irregular mounds, making the snow appear like icing on a wedding cake. She bumped her forehead against the glass. "I saved your life. If I hadn't come out there when I did, you would have frozen to death."

"Precisely. You went out there when you did."

"You think—" She couldn't breathe. Spots danced before her eyes, and she pressed a hand to her chest, gasping as though someone had knocked a fist into her solar plexus.

Because she had chosen to take a brief walk in the new-fallen snow, and he had decided to respond to a note she hadn't sent and take a longer walk to talk to her, he thought she had hit him over the head and then saved him from dying?

"Why?" She managed to choke out the single question that should have been several more. Why would she do that? Why would she save him? Why would she want him stranded at her house? Why would she risk everything in such a horrible way?

"It made more sense when I wasn't with you." He spoke from right behind her, and she jumped. He curved one hand around her shoulder. "I had to be honest with you about my hunt for the missing jewels always leading back to you."

"Your being struck in the head and left to perish in the snow leads you back to me?" Her shoulder shook beneath his hand. Her voice sounded thick, as though her high-boned lace collar were too tight. "I suppose that would make sense from your side of the matter. But I know I'm innocent and think perhaps there's someone else who is leading everything back to me."

"I wish I could think who." His tone was soft, gentle, and warm enough to melt the snow on the lawn below them. "Do you think I like thinking, even for a moment, that a lady as kind and lovely and generous as you is capable of harming me?"

"You think I'm capable of theft." Her words rasped past her lips when she wanted them to emerge with force.

"Will you give me evidence to prove me wrong?" He used a fingertip to gather tears from beneath her eyes, then he curved his hand around her cheek and turned her face toward him. "Please?"

"I don't know how." Through a veil of more tears, she gazed into his beautiful green eyes. Her mouth went dry. "You can't possibly want . . . to . . . to . . ."

But he could. He did. He smoothed his hand from her cheek to her chin, tilted it up, and kissed her.

She was a widow, and yet in those moments, doubted she had ever been kissed, especially not with such tender warmth. If she had, the action hadn't seared through her like sunshine melting the snow. Her knees wobbled, and she grasped his lapels for support. She inhaled his scent of something aromatic like thyme or rosemary. She tasted chocolate, and when he raised his head, she read something like wonder and confusion in his face, in the way he blinked slowly, gave his head a quick shake, and flicked his glance from her, to the windows, and back to her.

His lips parted, and she braced herself for the humiliation of his apology, his words of regret.

"I probably shouldn't have done that?" It sounded more like a query than a statement.

"It's rather improper."

"Rather." He shoved his hands into his coat pockets and looked past her again.

She drew her brows together and sighed. "Just say it, Lord Tristram. You're sorry you kissed me. You regret forgetting that I'm a lady and therefore untouchable." She forced a smile to her lips. "All right then. Apology accepted. Now, may we get back to the business at hand?"

"No, I do not think we can." He brushed a wisp of hair from her cheek. "My lady—Catherine—I regret a number of interactions in our brief acquaintance. I regret having to investigate you for the missing jewelry. I regret thinking for one second you were behind the incident last night. But I do not regret kissing you."

Speech and coherent thought abandoned her. She wanted nothing more than to wrap her arms around him and rest her head on his shoulder. She wanted to have him hold her and assure her they would find the person who was truly guilty. She wanted him to take her home, despite home to him being another English manor. She wanted to forget she would then be stealing yet another beau from Georgette and causing further trouble for her family.

Estelle burst into the conservatory with her banjo tucked under one arm and kept Catherine from doing anything more stupid than she already had.

"I'm sorry I kept you all waiting, but Florian sent around a message . . . asking . . ." Estelle trailed off and glanced from Tristram to Catherine then back again before grinning. "Did I interrupt something?"

"Nothing that cannot be renewed later." Tristram bowed. "How do you do, Miss VanDorn."

"Quite well, thank you, but you look rather wobbly. Perhaps you should sit down."

"If you ladies will join me." He stepped back so Catherine could precede him.

Cheeks too warm for Estelle not to notice, Catherine stumbled back to the sofa and collapsed onto the cushions. She picked up the chocolate pot to pour, felt it tremble in her hand, and set it down again. "Will you do the honors, Estelle? You need practice."

"So do you." Estelle was practically choking on suppressed laughter. It danced in her eyes and emerged as too many little coughs. And sharp caught breaths.

"Are you going to entertain us?" Catherine demanded more than asked.

"I am." Estelle set a cup in front of Tristram. "So what brought you out in a snowstorm?"

Tristram settled beside Catherine, keeping a proper six inches away. "The end of the storm. I needed fresh air after nearly a week in the city."

"But do you not work in the city?" Estelle settled on the seat adjacent to Tristram.

"You work?" Catherine posed the question before she realized how foolish she sounded.

She had let him kiss her—and she had kissed him back—but she knew far too little about him. It wasn't the sort of behavior Mama had instilled in her. It was the sort of behavior that had given her a reputation for being fast and caused her to end up in an English prison called a manor house.

"I don't know if I would call it work." Tristram shrugged off the subject. "A few other former officers and I work with men who were wounded in the Boer War and the Boxer Rebellion and help them find work, get their pensions, or learn new trades if they can't do the old ones. Most of them end up in the London stews, so that's where we go."

"How kind of you." Catherine gazed at him in awe. "I wish I'd known you when I was in England. I could have helped you raise money. I'm getting quite adept at organizing charity events."

"When you were in England, I was on my way home from South Africa in disgrace. This operation is rather new, and my father has been generous." He ducked his head, but failed to hide the flush of color along his sculptured cheekbones. "I expect to make up for my failure as an officer."

"That's not what I heard it was." Estelle exchanged her teacup for the banjo she had tucked behind her chair and began to pluck idly at the strings. "Ambrose told me—"

"A great deal of balderdash, I expect." Tristram raised a hand to the cowlick near the top and back of his head, right above where he had been struck the night before.

"Estelle," Catherine said in haste, "why do you not entertain us from farther away. You tend to get a little loud."

"Especially once Florian gets here." She rose, still playing, and strolled to another grouping of chairs on the other side of the room.

Catherine touched Tristram's arm. "Do you need to return to your room?"

"Not yet." He clasped her hand and, still holding her fingers, lowered it to the cushion between them. "We need to talk."

"We do." Her fingers trembled beneath his. "Your father will take away the funds to your charity if you don't find the jewel thief."

"Yes, and more." He tried to flatten his cowlick again. "Even if I inherit, if my brother's widow bears another girl, Father will give her all the money and property not entailed to the title. I will have an enormous estate to run without the money to run it."

"How irresponsible of him."

"Indeed." He removed his hand from his head. The cowlick sprang back into a tiny corkscrew curl, and Catherine fought the urge to reach up and smooth it herself. "I can guess how many people that is."

"Nearly a hundred people potentially punished because my father is so ashamed of me he can see nothing but how to hurt me."

She extracted her hand from his hold. "Thus you need an heiress in the event you were so concentrated on finding me guilty you didn't look for the true culprit."

"It's not like that, Catherine. If you think that's why I kissed you, you're wrong."

"You thought you could lure me into revealing my secrets?"

"I thought I could do something I've wanted to do since you walked into that ballroom and got everyone staring at your purple dress. You were so reckless, so defiant, so scared, I wanted to know your secrets."

"If only I had some to tell." She crossed her arms over her chest. "I don't. Everyone knows my husband neglected me. Everyone knows that old Mrs. Selkirk has convinced everyone she can that I, and thus my family, am too immoral for the good people of the Tuxedo Club to receive."

"And hasn't been particularly successful."

"This is a small enough community that that is enough to hurt Mama and bar Estelle from certain gatherings where she should be seen."

"I do not think she cares."

Estelle perched on a chair with her head tilted back, her eyes closed, and her fingers moving over the strings in a blur. She looked anything but distressed that she wasn't the belle of the season her elder sister had been.

"She saw how little good it has done me." Catherine fumbled in the pocket of her skirt for a handkerchief. It was black-bordered, as were all her handkerchiefs after Sapphire had sewn the edges on upon Bisterne's death, and Catherine hadn't purchased more.

Before she could apply it to her wet eyes, Tristram took it from her and exchanged it for a larger linen square, plain white save for his initials picked out in the same green as his eyes—TBW.

"Black doesn't suit you." He tucked her handkerchief into his coat pocket.

Catherine dabbed at her eyes. "What is the *B* for?"

"Baston-Ward."

Catherine jerked around to face him again. "The connection is closer than I thought. You're Florian's cousin?"

"And yours by marriage. Very distantly."

"So there's more to this jewel-hunting than your father's old friend needing aid."

"It's my mother's family. Whatever else one might say about my father as a loving, forgiving parent, he loved my mother." He removed Catherine's handkerchief from his pocket and began to fold and refold it. "He's been different since she died, less patient, less forgiving of human frailty, which I, according to him, have in an overabundance."

"Because you chose to leave the army?"

"No, my dear." He crushed the linen between his fingers. "I didn't decide to leave. I disliked the service, but it was my duty as the second son, so I took it. I ended up in South Africa and . . ." He pressed down the curl. "I was allowed to leave rather than be court-martialed."

∽◎

Her face paled and tightened, and Tristram suppressed a twisted smile. He was used to that action of withdrawal, the polite remoteness. A man wounded and leaving the military because of it was one thing. One allowed to resign his commission out of respect for his father's title and the number of Wolfes and Baston-Wards who had served before him, was quite something else. A pending court-martial meant he had let his country down.

She would regret kissing him now, if she didn't already. And of course she did already. Her remark about him needing an heiress spoke that thought loud and clear, though only moments earlier she had looked utterly besotted—the way he felt. It had distracted them both from the thoughtless way he accused her of bashing him over the head in the snow. He shouldn't have spoken that suspicion aloud. The evidence was only circumstantial.

All the evidence against her was circumstantial, from the jewels disappearing from the safe at Bisterne to them showing up in every European city she had visited. As with the jewels, who else would have been abroad to strike him down? The sort of persons who set about robbing guests of club members did not get inside the fence, let alone wander about in snowstorms.

Besides, she cared about him. She had learned how to control her outward expression of emotions well, but not perfectly. Even as she lashed back at his accusations, she looked hurt, not angry; she felt longing, not contempt.

Until now, when the blow on his head must have weakened him enough to tell her the truth. Or perhaps him giving in to the wish to kiss her had loosened his tongue into being truthful with her about everything. It was a gamble, and her arms crossed over her chest and taut face told him he'd lost.

"Insubordination, not cowardice." He may as well get it all out. "It was a horrible, unnecessary, and unjust war, and I despised my superior officers for how they were treating the people of the country. They herded them into camps like animals. Sheep ready for the slaughter were treated better. So I refused to destroy the village I was ordered to subdue and let everyone escape to safety. One of them thanked me with a blow to my head, which truly was a gift. It gave the army a reason to let me resign."

The liquid notes of Estelle's banjo filled the silence between Catherine and Tristram like water seeking a channel between two rocks. Catherine stared at him with those wide eyes that made him want to drown in their fathomless depths. His mouth dry, he reached for his chocolate, now cold with a skin of milk clotting the surface.

"Don't drink that. I'll ring for more." She jumped up so quickly electricity crackled from her wool skirt against the velvet cushion.

He reached out with some notion of stopping her, but let his hand fall. If she wanted to use serving a guest as an excuse to get away from him, the disgraced officer, then he would not stop her.

She rang the bell. As she gave her orders to the footman who appeared, the doorbell chimed.

Estelle stopped playing mid-arpeggio and sprang to her feet. "Florian is here."

Tristram glanced at her face, which glowed as though electric lights burned behind it, and felt a groan rise in his chest. She had fallen for Florian, a talented musician and an apparently good young man, but who possessed no money and fewer prospects without the jewels. That

Estelle was an heiress made the situation worse. Her parents would never approve of this match after Catherine's experience.

He needed to find the jewels or what had happened to them and get Florian back to England and out of harm's way—harm for Estelle. Yet how could he call on Catherine if she now rejected him?

He turned toward the head of the steps. Florian came into view with Ambrose right behind him.

"Look what the cat dragged in." Florian gestured behind him. "A veritable throng to comfort you, Tris."

He wasn't gesturing solely at Ambrose. Two more people reached the point where the steps flared to open into the conservatory.

Pierce and Georgette Selkirk swept up the last two steps, bright-cheeked and brighter-eyed and reminding Tristram of the bargain he had struck with Georgette and another reason why he could not call on Catherine.

CHAPTER 10

"The custom of raising the hat when meeting an acquaintance derives from the old rule that friendly knights in accosting each other should raise the visor for mutual recognition in amity. In the knightly years, it must be remembered, it was important to know whether one was meeting friend or foe. Meeting a foe meant fighting on the spot. Thus, it is evident that the conventions of courtesy not only tend to make the wheels of life run more smoothly, but also act as safeguards in human relationship."
Emily Price Post

The sight of Georgette, as bright as the sunshine melting snow from the roof, sent a shockwave of guilt racing through Catherine. Here she was, ready to beg forgiveness for the past, a goal she had strived for nearly since she left America, and she had kissed yet one more of Georgette's beaux not a half hour ago. Given warning of Georgette's arrival, she might have run away to hide her shame.

Not given warning, she stepped forward to extend her hands in welcome. "You chose a cold day for making calls." Not an auspicious greeting. "I mean . . . That is—"

Georgette interrupted with her sparkling laughter. "We just got back from the city, and I needed a guarantee that neither Mama nor Grandmother would want to stir from the drawing room fire."

The two of them stood a dozen feet apart, eyeing one another, while the others watched the tableau unfold. Georgette looked as young and golden as she had five years earlier. Her complexion and hair glowed in the lamplight. Her well-cut gown emphasized the lithe lines of her form. Best of all, her smile was as wide and warm as it had been all their years of friendship.

Wishing she were wearing something finer than a dark gray walking suit with only the narrowest bands of lace to adorn her collar, Catherine took the first step forward, then another. Georgette mirrored her actions. They met in the center of the Persian carpet to hug one another, neither speaking, neither moving. Tears welled in Catherine's eyes. Georgette had come to her when she was the wronged party. She tried to say something appropriate to the moment, but her throat swelled closed, blocked by too many words she had considered saying over the past five years.

In the doorway, a footman gave a discreet cough.

Catherine stepped back, blinking hard, to indicate he and a fellow servant should set the fresh chocolate and tea services on the low table between the sofas. The servants' presence gave Catherine time to compose herself and dab at her eyes with her handkerchief—no, Tristram's handkerchief. When she pulled the linen away, Georgette was seated facing the lake, where Tristram had been. He had joined the others on the other side of the room. Estelle held court there, dispensing chocolate and tea and making everyone laugh.

Georgette perched on the edge of the cushion, her feet together, her hands in her lap, and her cheeks damp, but her smile was firmly in place. "I always loved this room."

"It's my favorite." Catherine took up the chocolate pot. "Though I suppose I should have asked if you prefer tea now."

"Tea. But no sugar. I get plump if I'm not careful."

Catherine emitted an unladylike snort. "I find that difficult to believe."

"It's true. If I didn't walk miles a day on these hills or play tennis, I would look like a snowball in a white dress." Georgette accepted the teacup. "I rather overindulged myself with sweets after . . ." She trailed off. Her gaze flicked to Catherine, then down to her tea.

"After I eloped with your fiancé?" Catherine opened the door as wide as it could go. Her hands shook, and she left her cup on its saucer.

Across the room, Florian was trying to play Estelle's banjo, while the others groaned and laughed in warm camaraderie.

Catherine took a deep breath and plunged into her speech. "Georgette, this is still likely not enough to make up for the humiliation and pain I caused you and your family, but I have to tell you that he wasn't worth a moment of your grief. He wanted nothing more than the money. He wasn't the least bit interested in me once that ring was on my finger and my dowry was in his bank account."

"So I heard." Georgette turned her blue eyes fully on Catherine. "People from here visited London and sometimes saw him. Apparently he acted as though he barely remembered your name." She set her cup on the table and leaned forward. "At first, I thought it was the least you deserved. I couldn't bear to go out in public for weeks because I hated the sympathetic looks. And a few young men . . ." Her cheeks flushed. "They thought they could take advantage of my jilted state, if you understand what I'm saying."

"I do. Those same sort treated me like that after I was widowed."

They exchanged sympathetic glances, their own fragile camaraderie starting to take hold.

"He took me to that moldering old house of his," Catherine continued, "then left for London, where he stayed most of the time." She plucked at the smooth wool of her skirt. "But all that doesn't make up for what I did to you in luring him away. And I, well, I beg your forgiveness for putting such a shallow desire for a title before our friendship."

Speech delivered, Catherine sagged back against the sofa cushions and waited for relief, for the peace that had eluded her for over five years. Instead, her stomach felt as though she had consumed six cups of coffee.

No, not coffee, just an inappropriate closeness with the man behind her by a dozen feet. His voice, though no louder than the others, rang through her head clear and smooth and wound her insides like a seven-day clock. The longer Georgette remained silent, the tighter the tension grew.

Georgette remained so silent, the conversation of the others began to falter. Then, when Florian's inexpert plucking of the banjo strings was the only sound in the conservatory, she grasped the silver tongs, dropped a lump of sugar into her tea, and began to stir. "Carry on." She spoke without looking at the others.

They burst into a cacophony of conversation.

Georgette snorted and fixed her attention on Catherine. "At first, I hated you. I rather hoped your ship would sink in the middle of the Atlantic."

Catherine flinched, but wasn't truly surprised. She expected she would have felt the same in reverse.

"Then when I heard all wasn't like a fairytale for you," Georgette continued, "I thought it was what you deserved and thought if he'd married me, he wouldn't have treated me that way. Rather arrogant of me, isn't it?" She laughed, sipped some of her tea, and smiled. "I forgive you, Catherine. I forgave you a long time ago. At first it was just what I knew was the right thing to do, and then it was genuine."

"Thank you." Still, relief and peace eluded Catherine. "But why— Georgette, I have to ask—why have you never married? Surely you haven't been pining for Edwin."

"Not Edwin. A man who, like me, wants to get away from all this." She swept her arm in an arc to indicate the world outside.

More likely their narrow world within the Tuxedo Club fence.

"I am so weary of seeing the same people at the same parties year after year. When I go into the city, I want to attend the less savory theaters, those productions the immigrants put on. I want to go to Coney Island in the summer and take a boat from the city to Lake Erie. Lord Bisterne represented all that to me. He would take me away to another world." For a moment, her eyes shimmered like a summer sky, then the light died and her shoulders sagged. "Pierce won't even let me sneak off with him. He's been to school in England and all over Europe, but he won't so much as take me downtown wearing a veil. I'm stranded here in Tuxedo Park most of the time with a mother and grandmother who are more bitter over my broken engagement than I am."

"And do their best to damage my family's reputation even now." Catherine sighed to lift the burden from her heart. "What will change things?"

Georgette moved her shoulders in a casual shrug. "Perhaps if I marry another title?" A half smile played around her lips.

Catherine opened her mouth to say, "If you meet one," and then realized that Georgette already had—Lord Tristram Wolfe, heir presumptive to the Marquess of Cothbridge, and heir apparent, direct heir, if his sister-in-law didn't bear a son.

Surely if she truly wanted to mend fences between the families and stop old Mrs. Selkirk's vicious tongue, Catherine would be happy for Georgette. She and Tristram seemed to be getting along well. But a weight the size of Coney Island's Elephantine Colossus seemed to be sitting on her chest.

"Should I be congratulating you?" she asked instead.

Should she scorn him for kissing her while Georgette believed they had an unofficial understanding? He should be forgiven for the reason behind his near court-martial, but perhaps that insubordination was a sign he was incapable of loyalty.

Across the room, he now held the banjo, and Estelle was showing him how to position his fingers.

"If you played another instrument," she was saying, "this might be easier."

"He used to play the piano," Florian said.

Just one more thing Catherine didn't know about him.

Eyes half closed, Georgette leaned toward Catherine and lowered her voice. "This is between Tristram and me, but we only pretend an interest so my mother and grandmother will stop fussing."

"Georgie." Catherine's heart leaped. "Is he not perfect for someone to take you away?"

"He would simply take me to another type of confined life." Georgette plucked at a bit of lint on her wool skirt. "I have little interest in the same things as he. Back in England, he works to help men wounded in those two wars the English have been involved in lately. Something like the Boer War in China?"

"South Africa. China was the Boxer Rebellion."

"Whichever it might be." Georgette shrugged off details. "Lots of men come home wounded and don't have a way to support themselves other than small pensions. Some don't even have homes, so he and some other former military men raise money to help them learn trades or get back to their old ones."

"So I understand."

"He won't say, but I think he's come over here to raise money for his charity because his father might not give him his inheritance."

So Georgette suspected the same of him as Catherine had. Did he kiss Georgette as well, a way to ensure he caught at least one heiress?

"I don't know any details of that, either," Georgette continued, "but something about him having incomplete business and his father being angry with him for leaving military service."

She apparently knew nothing of the court-martial.

"I should think it's his duty to his country to serve," Georgette said. "But he was wounded. Perhaps that makes continuing to serve difficult. It doesn't matter, since if he marries an heiress, he won't need to concern himself with a bit of money from his father. Marrying to help dozens or hundreds of men recover from the war is so much more noble than merely restoring an old house."

"Indeed it is." Catherine glanced out the windows to where the wind had risen, whipping the tree branches into a fury, and clouds, already dropping their overabundance of flakes, quickly replaced the blue sky. The lake lay still and flat beneath its layer of ice.

Catherine suddenly longed to be out there chasing those flakes with the wind yanking back her hood and tugging the pins from her hair. She wanted to howl with the elements, and she didn't quite know why. She was getting what she wanted—a renewal of friendship with Georgette, the first step to reconciliation between both families. She should be ecstatic. Georgette did not even have her sights set on Tristram. And yet her words reminded Catherine of how awful life as the bride of an English aristocrat could be.

"If he inherits the title," she began.

"Heaven forbid." Georgette shuddered, then giggled. "But enough of that. One day, and soon I think, the man I believe feels as I do will find the courage to break tradition, and we shall become very bohemian in the city or perhaps even out west."

"If it is what you want, I hope it happens." Catherine smiled upon her old friend, despite the ache in her heart that she had no idea what she wanted, only what she did not want.

"But enough about me." Georgette reached out her hand to Catherine. "Let us talk about you. I want to know every detail of your tour through Europe this past year."

"The freedom of being a widow was quite divine."

Catherine spoke of the wonders of the Continent, and from there they filled in details of the missing years between them. Georgette wanted to know all about life in an English country house—"It wasn't all bad, was it?"—and Catherine wanted to know what Georgette had heard about school friends from Mrs. Graham's Academy, who had married and moved away, or just moved away.

"I was lonely," Catherine admitted, "but never bored. I had acres of gardens to restore and beautiful horses to ride, and I liked helping the tenants. We had a measles outbreak one summer, and I nearly killed myself nursing sick children, but they all lived, and that was so very satisfying."

Georgette made a face of disgust. "You sound like Susan Lassiter. She went to college, if you can believe it. Someplace in Ohio. Oberlin, that was it. She is now studying to be a doctor at Johns Hopkins in Baltimore."

"That's astounding. Her parents let her?"

"She inherited money from her grandfather, and her parents couldn't stop her. But they sold their house here in the Park right after she left, and now they spend their summers in Bar Harbor and winters in Boston. I think they're ashamed of her."

"I'd be proud of my daughter for not being shallow."

As she had been. Perhaps as she still was, spending her days doing nothing more than planning a few charity engagements and what to wear to the next social gathering, trying to keep Estelle from thinking about running off to join a band with Ambrose or Florian, or sitting by a fire with her needlework while others gossiped around her. In her youth she had wanted nothing more than to be the most popular girl at a ball and marry a title. Once she had those, she realized she needed more, if only she knew what that "more" was.

"Susan wants to be a missionary," Georgette said. "She writes to me now and again. She is why I am inspired to get away from here. But I think I would be dreadful at the bedside of a sick person."

"I thought that once, but I slept well after a good day's work." Catherine stared into the sameness of her future as her life stood at the time. "Perhaps I should learn to be a nurse."

"You would break your mother's heart. But we can work on a charity event for the less privileged. I suppose you need no help with the Christmas tea, but something else will come along. We will buy a ticket for your tea, by the way, and I will make Pierce and Tristram come, as well. And for now . . ." Georgette rose. "I had better go home before the weather gets any worse. Grandmother predicted this, which is why we came home today. With Lord Tristram out here, she didn't want me stranded in the city." She glanced his way and giggled.

Flakes the size of quarters now chased one another from the pile of clouds to the ground, where they stuck.

"Thank you for coming." Catherine stood before her old friend. "I don't deserve your forgiveness."

"Of course you do. I would be in the wrong if I didn't give it."

They embraced again, and Georgette departed with her brother with admonitions to the Englishmen not to tarry and get stranded. Pierce was too polite not to bow to Catherine, but it was little more than an inclination of his head. He, apparently, was not ready to put the past behind him, just like his mother and grandmother. Until Georgette ended her charade of letting Tristram court her, or her secret beau broke his own chains, Catherine must maintain her distance.

What an absurd coil born of the many rules and regulations money had created rather than freed them from.

Ignoring the protests of the Englishmen and Estelle, Catherine crossed to the windows and flung open one of the casements to feel the blast of icy air in her face in lieu of a walk. Most of her heart felt at peace over the reconciliation with her old friend. The rest of her spirit twisted and turned like the snow trying to carpet the floor at her feet.

Georgette still did not trust Catherine enough to confide the name of her gentleman of like mind. Not all was healed. Possibly the only right action Catherine could take was to leave Tuxedo Park, and yet if she did, Tristram would believe that her guilt had driven her away.

She closed the window, faced the room, and met Tristram's eyes. Her knees nearly buckled beneath her. She could never look at him again without remembering the intensity of that kiss, and now a memory following—Edwin kissing her after a tennis match. They had played against Georgette and Paul Three and won. Heady with victory and the attentions of the English earl, Catherine had kissed him back with abandon. Two days later, they had eloped. Her father had released her dowry, reluctantly but unavoidably, and Edwin gave her the first of the jewels he claimed were not part of the Bisterne collection.

The jewels. Solving the riddle of their disappearance was the only way to protect herself from making another mistake with another Englishman in need of a rich heiress.

Catherine headed for the corridor to her room.

Tristram caught her hand as she passed him. "You aren't going to join us, my lady?"

"No." She drew her hand free before the contact of their fingers sent her heart racing even harder. "I shall return."

She sped to her room with more haste than grace and yanked the drawer out of her jewel case. After ensuring none of her personal jewelry was mixed in, she marched back to the conservatory and poured the gemstones into Tristram's lap.

The music ceased in midnote. Florian and Ambrose stared wide-eyed. Estelle's mouth dropped open.

Tristram merely arched one brow. "What is this lot?"

"Jewels Bisterne gave me. For all I know, they are glass or paste. I have had too little occasion to wear them to care." Catherine stepped back, clutching the empty drawer against her chest. "So be done with these accusations and leave me in peace."

Tristram bowed his head over the brooches, strands of beads, and bracelets, holding up each piece to the light while the others stared in silence. At last, he lifted his head, and clouds marred the clear green of his eyes. "I cannot, my lady. I have no idea from where these jewels were obtained, and not one was listed as among the missing pieces, and those are what I am commissioned to recover."

CHAPTER 11

"A young man walking with a young woman should be careful that his manner in no way draws attention to her or to himself. Too devoted a manner is always conspicuous, and so is loud talking. Under no circumstances should he take her arm, or grasp her by or above the elbow, and shove her here and there, unless, of course, to save her from being run over!" Emily Price Post

Four pairs of eyes bored into Tristram. Too late, he remembered that Estelle knew nothing of the stolen jewels, and Florian wanted her to remain ignorant for fear she would side with her sister and against him. Estelle's heightened color suggested Florian was right.

In contrast, Catherine had paled. She backed away from him as though he would grab her and haul her to prison or someplace equally unpleasant, then spun on her heel and stalked from the room.

"What," Estelle bit out, "is this all about?"

"Missing jewelry from the Bisterne estate." Ambrose sounded weary.

Florian groaned and lowered his head to grip with his hands.

"And you think my sister took them?" Estelle rose, snatched up her banjo, and towered over Tristram too close for him to rise. "How dare you! How dare any of you! My sister is kind and honest and gener-ous. She gives. She does not take." She too stalked from the room, but paused on the landing to fire over her shoulder, "And if she took the jewelry, she earned it rebuilding the house and nursing sick children for a man who abandoned her to go carouse with men like you, Ambrose Wolfe." She vanished from view, and a moment later, a door down the corridor slammed.

"That's torn it," Ambrose murmured.

"I think," Florian said, "you have just lost me the most beautiful, most precious lady I will ever meet."

"Do you not mean the richest?" Ambrose nudged Florian in the ribs.

Florian gave him a blank look. "Richest? I suppose she is."

Tristram stared at the jewels in his lap, certain Florian genuinely cared for Estelle and even more certain Cothbridge's only living son was going to live up to the marquess's expectations, those expectations being so low. In other words, he had gone about his investigation all wrong.

He was not supposed to like the lady. He should not have been so eager to be in her company that he responded to her note late in the evening and thus gotten himself bashed in the head. He should have been more circumspect in questioning her about the jewelry, not accuse her outright.

He should not have kissed her.

He suspected stronger men than he would have found resisting her luscious mouth difficult. He half expected her pink lips to taste like strawberries. The chocolate was sweeter, more intoxicating, an action to repeat.

But the circumstances pointed to her being a thief. She had no right to the jewelry even if she had used her money to rebuild the house, and her energy to nurse sick children.

Could a woman who nursed sick children be bitter enough to take what was not hers? The answer, the proof, apparently rested on his knees.

He picked up a string of amber beads. They were warm as though having recently graced her ladyship's long, slender throat.

"Are those part of the collection?" Ambrose asked.

"I need to check the list."

Tristram felt only a twinge of guilt over that falsehood. He had the list memorized. He already knew every one of the gems Catherine had dumped in his lap belonged in the vault at Bisterne.

"Just say they are and have an end to this." Florian surged to his feet and glared at the window as though the snow were responsible for the shambles of his love life. "There are only a few pieces missing now, aren't there?"

"A few pieces just short of being as valuable as the Crown Jewels," Ambrose pointed out. "And if just one of these pieces is on the list of missing jewelry, we have proof Lady Bisterne is a thief."

"Not if she thought they were legitimate gifts from her husband." Tristram began to stuff the pieces into his coat pockets.

Ambrose and Florian gazed at him with raised brows.

"You are giving up?" Ambrose's voice rang with accusation. "Your father will not approve."

"But Estelle will." Florian smiled.

"I wish I could." Tristram suddenly wanted to discover each piece in his pockets was artificial so he could drop them onto the tile floor and grind them beneath his heel. But he had learned much about gemstones in the past year and recognized the deep glow of the real thing when he saw it.

As much as he wanted to do so, if he walked away now, he would lose far too much—too much that would hurt other people.

He rose, a trifle shaky with his still-throbbing head. "I think the best course of action right now is to let her believe this ends the matter.

We will bide our time and look out for more pieces to appear in jewelry stores."

"And perhaps Estelle will forgive me if she thinks we are leaving her sister alone." Florian strode to the landing and gazed down the corridor, longing tightening his fine-boned features.

Ambrose snorted. "As if her parents will approve of a penniless nobody. He'd be better off—" He stopped.

Tristram turned to see a footman reach the landing. "Do you gentlemen need anything?" The servant glanced about as though seeking the ladies.

"Is it possible to provide us with transport back to the Selkirks'?" Tristram asked.

The footman hesitated. "The snow is light, but the road will be rather slick."

"I can drive them." A voice drifted from the lower floor. A moment later, Paul Three's head showed through the railing. "I'm the best driver in this household, though you know you all are welcome to stay."

Thinking of Georgette's glance of interest toward this man in Central Park, Tristram moved forward to meet Paul VanDorn on the landing. "I think we should go."

The footman hastened to gather Tristram's things from the guest room. Another servant collected hats and coats, and the four gentlemen set off for the Selkirk house on the lake with the odd name: Wee Wah.

The road was indeed slippery. Even at the snail's pace at which Paul Three drove, the back wheels of the auto took on a life of their own and threatened to land them in a ditch more than once. Were not his head still making him dizzy, Tristram would have felt far more comfortable walking. Once, they had to stop and push the vehicle to get it up the last part of the hill. But at last, they arrived in the Selkirk drive numb with cold. Happy he could perform a favor for someone, or at the least see if Paul shared Georgette's interest, Tristram invited him in to warm himself.

"I may not be welcome." Eagerness lent a sparkle to Paul's dark eyes.

Tristram grinned, certain he had his answer—an answer that absolved him of not courting Georgette as he knew Pierce expected him to do. Frowns on the faces of the older Selkirk ladies suggested Paul was not entirely welcome, yet even they would not turn a man out in the cold after he had driven their guests home. They absented themselves, while the rest of them enjoyed an afternoon of playing board games.

When warmer breezes drove the snow clouds away, Paul took his leave, and Georgette dragged Tristram into a sitting room. "Thank you, though I don't know how you knew."

"I had a few clues. But truly, Georgette, this feud has gone on too long. Paul is a perfectly acceptable match for you."

"Not yet." She kissed Tristram's cheek. "So do, please, keep up the charade a little longer."

He kept up the charade more for his sake than Georgette's. While she and Paul VanDorn could not make their interest in one another public, dancing attendance on Georgette kept Tristram in Tuxedo Park and away from Catherine.

In truth, he did not see her even from a distance for over a week. Another spate of warm weather descended on Tuxedo Park, and his party spent a great deal of time playing tennis at the club and picnicking near one of the lakes. Once they all motored out of the park and into the countryside. And almost every night, dancing took place somewhere. Tristram dutifully danced with Georgette and noted half a dozen times she disappeared afterward. He suspected she met Paul somewhere. Considering the VanDorn family never appeared at these parties, Tristram began to guess that the feud continued, and Georgette was not allowed to meet with Paul in a proper courtship.

The day the cold weather returned, he asked Georgette about it. "Is it not ridiculous?"

"It is, but his father disapproves of me as much as my mother disapproves of Paul."

"But why do you not simply marry? You are both past your majority."

"Money, Tris. Does it not always return to money?" Georgette blinked back tears. "If I wed against Grandmother's will, I do not receive my inheritance, and Paul doesn't receive his until he is twenty-five, even if he does marry."

"But I have heard he is an excellent businessman for all he is only twenty-three."

"And his father will see that no one in the city hires him if Paul leaves the VanDorn company." She seized Tristram's hands. "So you see how important your pretending to court me is? If I marry someone of whom Grandmother approves, someone like you, she will stop being so nasty about what Catherine did to me five years ago."

"But you are not going to marry me, and if you did, you could not marry Paul."

"I think this will all be over soon. My mother and Grandmother have decided to attend Mrs. VanDorn's Christmas charity tea this year. This is the first time they have bought tickets since before Catherine eloped. An excellent sign."

The first occasion at which Tristram was guaranteed to encounter Catherine.

His pulse kicked up in anticipation. He had learned that she was spending a great deal of time in the city. Disposing of more jewelry? He couldn't stop himself from wondering. Avoiding him, perhaps? She had reason to after he accused her of luring him into the snow, after further accusations of stealing gems from her husband's family, after he had kissed her.

Of all those missteps, he regretted two of them and wanted to repeat the third. But he had a mission to complete, and his time to do so was growing short.

The day before the day New York celebrated as Thanksgiving, Tristram received a telegram from his father.

YOU ARE WASTING YOUR TIME STOP THOUGHT YOU COULD AT LEAST SUCCEED IN THIS SIMPLE TASK STOP HOME BY FIRST OF YEAR REGARD-LESS STOP

He understood the summons. His sister-in-law was due for her lying-in around the first of the year, and if she bore another girl, the marquess needed to know how to change his will.

Tristram had a month to find an answer to take home. Even less when he considered the week needed to cross the Atlantic, if he could find a vessel headed the northern route that time of year. If not, he would have to cross farther south and take the overland route across the Continent.

If he didn't have answers, he may as well not bother to return.

But he didn't want to be a failure. He wanted to prove his father wrong about him, if just once. He doubted going home with an heiress wife would improve his father's opinion of him—the marquess would consider that cheating. If he didn't have the rest of the jewels, the money recovered from the sale of the jewels, or the name of the culprit, he may as well not go home at all.

Except he did have the name of the culprit—Catherine, Lady Bisterne. Yet not even the son of a British nobleman accused a dowager countess of theft without irrefutable proof. That she gave him a fistful of jewels from the Baston-Ward collection meant nothing. Her word would be accepted that her husband had given them to her as gifts. And a number of pieces were still missing.

Too restless to remain at the Selkirk house, Tristram descended the hill to the clubhouse. But once among the gentlemen of the Tuxedo Club, he discovered he was also too restless to sit and listen to talk of American politics with men he barely knew, so Tristram left the fireside and wandered to the window. More snow had fallen the night before, shining like the moon beneath lights spilling through the clubhouse windows. And across the glowing terrain, a woman glided. Briefly, an outside light shone on her face.

In an instant, Tristram was out the door. Finding her track was not difficult. Her tiny feet had left deep impressions in the snow, blurred from where her skirt dragged around her. The lady had foolishly chosen to cut a trail through the untouched snow along the woodland path rather than take the road. Tuxedo Park might be as safe as one's own garden, but she still shouldn't be out there alone at night. If she must walk alone at night, she should at least stick to the road.

Unless, of course, she had caught a glimpse of him on her way out of the clubhouse and was trying to avoid him.

"No such fortune, my lady." His mouth set, he followed the footprints, making no effort to quieten the crunch of his boot heels on the snow's glazed surface or fallen branches. He wanted to talk to her, not sneak up behind her and terrify her.

His strides longer than hers, he caught a glimpse of her in a few minutes, a graceful figure in dark wraps taking measured steps in the as yet untouched whiteness. She had to hear him, but she neither sped up nor slowed. He considered the idea of calling to her to stop, then rejected it. She probably knew these woods. He didn't want her going to great lengths to avoid him and cut into some overgrown path where she could lose him and risk losing herself if she took a tumble and no one found her for days.

At last, he closed the distance between them and slipped his hand beneath her elbow. "Did you think you could avoid me forever in a closed community like this one?"

"I intended to give it a valiant attempt." She removed her arm from his hold. "I still do."

"Even though that means breaking your word?"

She said nothing. Starlight blazing through the bare tree branches sparkled on the puff of frosty breath from between her pursed lips. They had to be cold. Temperatures ranged well below freezing, bringing to mind how warm her lips could be, had been, should be.

He jerked his gaze away to the dim path before them. "You told me you would be at home to receive me if I persuaded Georgette to come calling on you and mend fences. Now the whole family is coming to your charity tea. I better than upheld my end of the bargain. Now it is your turn, and you're failing."

"I made that promise before you persisted in treating me like a criminal, accusing me of bashing you on the head as well as continuing to harbor stolen jewels. Now please leave me." She gathered her hood around her face—and tripped over a branch across the track.

Tristram caught her elbow to keep her from falling. She murmured her thanks and kept walking.

"I know about Georgette's plans." He tucked Catherine's arm against his side. The action warmed him.

She tensed as though intending to pull away again, then relaxed. "Do you not mean her feelings for you she covers up with some balderdash about having a *tendre* for some other man?"

"That is no cover, my lady. Georgette is in love with your brother."

She checked her stride. "But Paul is a year younger than she is and too quiet and obedient for someone who will please Georgette."

"Then apparently you do not know your brother."

"*Touché.*" She puffed out a sigh. "I haven't had a conversation with him since he left for Harvard. But if he and Georgette want to wed, they should wed."

"Not without parental permission."

He felt her flinch.

"So I have even more to answer for." Her voice sounded thick. "I ran off with her fiancé, so her grandmother has done her best to ruin my family socially, which in turn has angered my father enough he won't allow Paul Three to court Georgette."

"And what else . . . Catherine?"

"Nothing." Her cry rang out in the quiet woodland. "I am not guilty of stealing jewelry or bashing you on the head. Why can you not believe me? I returned those pieces I thought I had a right to."

The trees broke at a meadow, and he paused to face her. "I want to believe you, Catherine, but the evidence says otherwise."

"Including me trying to kill you in the snow?"

"As to that . . ." He puffed out a long breath, forming a cloud between them. "I find that difficult to believe, but who else has reason to harm me?"

"The real thief, if the other gemstones are real."

"What I have been able to recover are real enough."

"Except for the combs that were my wedding gift from Edwin." Her laugh sounded as brittle as icicles hanging from the trees.

And like the tip of one of those cold spears, her hurt sliced through Tristram. The last thing he wanted was to hurt her further. Yet how could he get to the truth and make matters right back home if he did not press her?

Aching, he raised a gloved hand to touch her cheek. "If Bisterne even knew the jewels were artificial."

She gave him a quick, sharp glance but did not remove his hand. "What do you mean?"

"How much did he have to do with the jewels?" He slipped his fingers beneath her chin, tilting it up so the starlight illuminated her face and shone in her dark eyes. "Did he go into the safe?"

"Let me think." The tip of her tongue darted out to moisten her lower lip. "I never saw him take anything out. He only went into the safe on one of the quarter days to safeguard the rents until the next time he went into town to the bank."

"Which was when?"

"Michaelmas last year."

"And the jewels were there then?"

"I saw them. It was like Aladdin's cave. He opened all the cases and looked at them as usual. He asked me—" A noise somewhere between a gasp and a sob caught at her voice, and her head drooped, dislodging his hand. "He asked me if I had any parties to which I wanted to wear any of them. Then he laughed and closed up the safe. Later that day, he took the train up to London, and the next day, Ambrose took the train back down to Bisterne to tell me Edwin was . . . gone. I never touched the safe."

"I'm sorry." Tristram clasped both her hands. "I knew Edwin was neglectful of you. I didn't know he was cruel."

"I paid my dues for taking him away from Georgette. Yet everyone is still making me pay for my youthful folly."

Suddenly she stopped, stooped, and came up with both hands full of snow. While Tristram watched in fascination, she formed the handsful of snow into a ball the size of a pineapple and threw it against the nearest tree as hard as she could. The snow missile exploded in a puff of white, and she followed it with another and another to emphasize her words. "My family has been shunned by several hostesses." Explosion. "I have to endure old Mrs. Selkirk telling me with whom I can and cannot associate." Explosion. "And I dare not disobey for all I'm twenty-four." Explosion. "And a widow." Explosion. "And my trust fund can buy and sell the Selkirks twice over. And if you don't stop laughing, I will—"

The final explosion struck him squarely on the chin. Snow filled his mouth, shot up his nose, and managed to slip between his muffler and neck. Shock of the impact knocked him back a step. He slipped in the white stuff and ended up sitting in the snow, still laughing.

"Are you all right?" Catherine transformed back to her staid persona and dropped to her knees beside him. "I didn't mean to—I never should have—" She raised her hand to his face and brushed away the snow.

He caught hold of her fingers and held them to his cheek. "It's quite all right, my dear. But if it's a snowball fight you want, give me the opportunity to arm myself and make it fair."

She backed away. "I don't think that would be proper for a dowager countess."

"Nor is walking through the woods alone at night, but you were doing it." He gathered handsful of snow as he scrambled to his feet. "Nor do they have tantrums, yet you did. Nor do they throw snowballs at the sons of peers, yet you did." On the last word, he lobbed the packed snow at her, aiming for her shoulder.

It struck just high enough to knock back her hood and probably send snow sliding beneath her collar. She shrieked, grabbed snow from the top of a drift and shot it back.

And the battle was on. They packed, they threw, they caught missiles on their upraised arms, their torsos, and in their hands. To Tristram's chagrin, Catherine was a better shot than he was. Where he lacked in accuracy, he made up for in speed. He kept her darting from tree to tree.

Finally she collapsed against one, her hands on her knees where snow encrusted her gown, breaths whooping in and out of her lungs. "Uncle. Uncle."

He'd never heard the expression, but got the message. Out of breath himself, he closed the distance between them and took her hands to lift her upright. "I didn't hurt you, did I?"

"Only my pride that I had to surrender." She tilted her head back. The pure oval of her face glowed in the starlight-and-snow ambiance. Her eyes danced with laughter. Her mirth faded into the night, but her lips remained parted, forming a trail of vapor guiding his mouth to hers.

In an instant, their cold lips warmed. Her hair had come loose in their play, and he buried his fingers in the thick mane, cupping the back of her head. With her fingers tangled between his muffler and the back of his neck, he thought he might be happy remaining thus in contact with her for minutes or hours.

But cold began to seep from his feet up, and he could not risk her well-being for a few moments of bliss.

With reluctance, he drew her hood over her tumbled locks and drew away. "I seem to like doing that."

She crossed her arms over her chest. "Even though I'm a criminal?"

"Because everything about you except for the evidence says you cannot be a criminal." Yearning to kiss her again, he settled for one gloved finger across her lips. "Because you nursed sick children on farms. Because you still feel guilty for hurting your friend even though it no longer matters to her. Because I never know what you are going to do next, whether it is dumping a pile of jewels in my lap or throwing snowballs at me."

"Or luring you into the snow so I can bash you on the head and leave you to freeze." She turned her head away from his touch. "With that accusation coming from your lips, your pretty speech makes your kiss taste like poison."

"Catherine. My lady." Words failed Tristram, and he swallowed a roughness in his throat. "Let me take you home." His voice was a mere rasp.

She nodded and tucked her hand into the crook of his elbow. They headed out in silence save for the rhythmic crunching of their footfalls driving the accusation into his spirit, *You're despicable. Despicable. Despicable . . .*

Going home without absolute proof of Catherine's guilt would be worse than humiliating. He would have to admit to his father that he had too much regard for the lady, too much attraction to her, to seek that proof, or simply lay the evidence gathered in his father's lap and let him take over. The courts would listen to the Marquess of Cothbridge. That marquess would see Catherine perhaps punished as far as prison and see his son punished as far as left penniless or even tossed to the mercy of the court-martial after all.

"We need to talk about this further, Catherine," he spoke at last.

"I will talk all you like if I can convince you of my innocence."

He felt as if she had just bestowed a gift upon him.

"Thank you." He indulged himself with the merest brush of his lips on her cheek, then waited for the butler to let her into the house before he strode down the drive and up to the Selkirk house. He retired for the night with the befuddlement of a man torn between longing for the lady to be his and fearing her guilt could no longer be avoided.

He knew he was only fooling himself to say no one would believe her guilt. With the evidence he had gathered presented to the Marquess of Cothbridge, she would be condemned before a barrister tried to defend her. He could make his father happy in a moment, with words in a telegram.

And make himself and Catherine miserable for the rest of their lives.

"What if she is innocent?" He spoke the query aloud to his empty bedchamber.

Toss and turn and try as he might, he could not think how. Yet he would struggle for evidence in her favor, for another culprit.

Sometime after midnight, he fell asleep with this determination and woke to a day of a special church service, gathered family and friends, and much eating, while the temperature dropped. The following morning proved to be the coldest morning he had ever experienced. High winds blasted sheets of ice against the windows. It was the kind of morning that drove everyone to the dining room warmed by a blazing fire to drink gallons of coffee. None wanted to leave the cozy room to so much as retrieve a book from the library. They indulged in idle chitchat about the entertainments offered for when more snow fell and the ice froze solid on the lakes, what they would do for Christmas, and who would brave the chill in the hall to fetch them a game or something to read. No one wanted to force the servants away from the warmth of the kitchen.

"I will go." Tristram rose and stepped into the foyer. Frigid drafts swirled around him. On his way across the marble tiles to the library, he passed a refectory table against one wall. A pile of mail rested on a silver tray waiting for one of the Selkirks to collect and sort. Tristram picked it up, thinking he would carry it to Pierce, and noted his name on a small parcel that had come by courier, not the United States Postal Service.

Reading the handwriting on the paper, he thought the draft had found its way to his heart, chilling it into stopping. With clumsy fingers, he tore off the plain wrapping and opened the box within.

One of the New York jewelers he had contacted with drawings of the missing jewels had borne him fruit by collecting and sending one of the Baston-Ward pieces. A scrawled note at the bottom of the bill said *Sold to me by a lady of average height and excellent form wearing black and a thick veil. Tried to follow, but she disappeared into a waiting cab.*

CHAPTER 12

"Therefore, it is of the utmost importance always to leave directions at the door such as, 'Mrs. Jones is not at home,' 'Miss Jones will be home at five o'clock,' 'Mrs. Jones will be home at 5.30,' or 'Mrs. Jones "is at home" in the library to intimate friends, but "not at home" in the drawing-room to acquaintances.' It is a nuisance to be obliged to remember either to turn an 'in' and 'out' card in the hall, or to ring a bell and say, 'I am going out,' and again, 'I have come in.' But whatever plan or arrangement you choose, no one at your front door should be left in doubt and then repulsed. It is not only bad manners; it is bad housekeeping." Emily Price Post

The Selkirks' automobile caught up with Tristram when he was only a quarter of the way to the VanDorns. The chauffeur was driving the housekeeper into the village and stopped to invite him to ride to his destination. Already weary of the now ice-coated snow alongside the road and the slicing wind, Tristram climbed aboard.

As he descended a few minutes later, he trudged up the drive of Lake House, too slick for the automobile, and reached the door feeling as though the pearl-and-diamond earrings in his pocket weighed as many pounds as they were worth in British pounds. He could scarcely raise his hand to press the doorbell.

The supercilious butler opened the portal. To the strains of a cello in the distance, he swept his faded blue gaze up and down, and shook his head. "I am sorry you came out in this weather, my lord. Lady Bisterne is not at home."

"I believe you must be mistaken." Tristram prepared to shove his foot in the door to keep the butler from shutting it in his face. "She told me last month she would be."

And not being at home was as good as a confession, was it not? He had agonized for three days to wait for this afternoon. Seeing her in church, he nearly shook Georgette off his arm in order to plow through the crowd to Catherine.

"She did not inform me as such." The door came toward him.

Tristram inserted his foot and leaned his shoulder against the massive oak panel. "Do, please, take her my card." He extracted one from his pocket and pressed it into the butler's gloved hand. "I can wait inside here." He stepped over the threshold.

The butler could either stand there with the door open, or close it and seek out Catherine.

He chose the latter, stalking off like a thwarted three-year-old. His heavy footfalls took him in the drawing room with its music room beyond. A moment later, the cello ceased and was replaced by the low rumble of a voice.

"Of course she's at home." Miss Estelle's voice rose loud and clear, growing louder. "This subterfuge is completely poor management and such bad form." She arrived in the foyer still carrying her bow. "Lord Tristram, I'm sorry you've been kept standing here in the cold of the corridor. Do come into the library where you can get some warmth. Catherine's edict to not be disturbed doesn't apply to you." She swept around in an arc and strode off for a door down the hall, her skirt flounces bobbing.

Tristram didn't deign to so much as glance the butler's way before following Estelle to the library door.

Estelle didn't bother to knock. She twisted the handle and flung the portal wide. "You are at home to Lord Tristram, are you not? Don't say no. He's right here." She gestured for him to precede her into the chamber.

Warmth from the air greeted him on the threshold. The mere sight of Catherine warmed him inside.

Until she looked up from a sheaf of mail before her and her face tightened. "I said not to be disturbed under any circumstances. The vocalist for Mrs. Henry's charity soirée has come down with some ailment and cannot perform. Now I have three days to find a replacement."

"You need look no further," Estelle said, and left the room, closing the door behind her.

Catherine sighed and fixed her gaze on Tristram. "Mama takes a day to rest, and the household staff forgets its direction. In other words, why were you let in?"

"Your butler had no choice." He closed the distance between them and stood gazing down at her, his heart aching. "Catherine, you cannot avoid me."

She rose. "I would prefer to."

"Why? Because of items like these?" He drew a box from his pocket, flipped off the lid, and set it on the desk between them.

She glanced down at the earrings, and her face paled. "Where did they come from?"

"A jeweler in New York, two days after you were in the city."

Something like a groan escaped her lips, and she closed her eyes. "And you think I am so foolish I would sell them this close to home knowing you are looking for them?"

"No, I don't. It's too much of a coincidence, but you're the only person who can help me learn the truth."

Her eyes widened. "You believe I'm innocent at last?"

"Yes." He hesitated. "Mostly."

She scowled.

He held out his hand. "You will help me."

"I told you everything I know. Except—" She drew one of the earrings from the box and scraped her teeth along a pearl.

Tristram shuddered. He had tried that trick himself.

"I should have done this with those combs." Catherine dropped the earring into the box. "If they were artificial on our honeymoon, I would have prepared for a disastrous marriage."

"I am sorry." Tristram rounded the desk to stand beside her. He would remember he was a gentleman and not touch her, but he needed to be near her, inhaling her spring-flower scent, lending her comfort with his nearness.

"For what? I made my bed, and it was as uncomfortable as I deserved."

"You cannot continue to castigate yourself for what you did five years ago." He could not stop himself from taking one of her hands between both of his. "You paid your dues."

"Not according to too many people here who are in the Selkirk camp. Georgette is so beloved, so sweet, that I would hurt her as I did condemns me in most people's eyes, and I cannot shake that off. And if our servants learn you were here and pass that along to other servants, the vitriol will continue. I will once again be accused of trying to steal Georgette's beau."

"But I am not her beau."

"Everyone thinks you are. They don't know you think me a thief."

"So my little charade with Georgette has hurt you." Tristram wanted to crawl under the desk for shame.

Catherine drew her hand free and turned her back on him, though she moved only a pace away. "I know you think it has been to help her, and who doesn't want to? She is unhappy here with that bitter old woman ordering her life because she still holds the purse strings. And

I can't expose the charade for what it is and hurt her again until she is ready."

"I never should have agreed to it, but at the time, I thought it the best way to remain here."

"And pin a theft on me." She raised her fingertips to her temples and pressed. "Now I cannot help you, my lord."

"Catherine." He reached one hand out to her, then let it drop without meeting its goal. "I need you. I mean, I need you to help me."

But in those misspoken words, he knew he needed her for more than her aid in discovering the true culprit—he needed her in his life. Yet his determination to prove her guilty had likely destroyed any hope of a future with her.

He heaved a sigh that felt like it rose from the depths of his soul. "There is no honor in what I have done. I know my intentions are good, but I am now not certain the end justifies the means by which I have gone about trying to achieve it."

At last, she faced him. "You did what you thought was right. But you need to unwind the coil you've gotten yourself into, and I am not a part of it. I am not guilty of theft. I know no more than I have told you, but if something else occurs to me, I will inform you."

"Catherine, please." He gazed into her wide, dark eyes and could not resist laying one hand against her cheek. Her skin was as smooth and cool as porcelain. He wanted to warm it, bring color into her face. He stroked her face, heartened when she did not jerk away. "I am truly sorry—"

The library door burst open. "Catherine, Lord Tristram, do come join the rest and listen to my new composition. We can—oh." Estelle's voice broke off.

Catherine startled back. Her face paled, and her hand flew to her lips.

Tristram turned slowly to face a veritable throng in the doorway—Estelle and Ambrose, Florian and Pierce and Georgette.

She was rather good at organizing everyone's life but her own. In the month since she returned to Tuxedo Park, she had organized three charity events, taken over much of the household management from Mama, and ensured Estelle attended at least half of the social events to which she was invited. The busier she was, the less she thought about how Edwin had hurt her, how Tristram did not entirely believe her innocent of stealing the Baston-Ward jewels, how badly she wanted to throw herself into his arms and have him kiss her until she could no longer think. She should not have let his touch linger on her face, but took it as a consolation for all she was giving up in the name of healing relations between herself and Georgette and between the families. Charade or not, she must go along with Georgette's pretend courtship with Tristram. With her family and the people of Tuxedo Park lay Catherine's future, not Lord Tristram Wolfe.

Yet there stood everyone staring at her with accusatory glares, and she was back five years to when the telegrams and letters spilled across the Atlantic, the vitriol pouring over her for her actions in running off with the best catch of the season.

So, as too often occurred, she needed to repair one deceit with another. Snatching her handkerchief from her pocket, she dabbed at her eyes. "Forgive me. I must be overtired to be so upset over the loss of an earring." In haste, she spun on her heel and snatched the diamond-and-pearl bauble she had tested with her teeth moments earlier off the desk and into her handkerchief. "But this tea party is in only two days and will not organize itself." Tucking the handkerchief into her pocket with the earring, she cast a smile to Georgette. "Do you think you can spare the time to help with the seating arrangements?"

"I think I'd like that." Georgette took a tentative step through the doorway.

"You don't want to go home, Georgie?" Pierce asked.

"No, I'll stay." She moved more quickly to the desk.

Tristram paced in the opposite direction, heading toward the others. "I'd like to go back with you, Pierce."

"Stay and listen to one piece," Estelle urged. "I call this one 'Joy.'"

They all departed. Catherine swept the other earring into a desk drawer and drew the lists for the tea to the center of the desk.

But Georgette had moved to the mantel to gaze at a grouping of photographs. She selected one from the crowd. From over her shoulder, Catherine noted it was the one of them bundled in hats and scarves to the point they were barely recognizable. Georgette sat in a skating chair with Catherine behind prepared to push her across the frozen lake.

"We had so much fun together as girls, didn't we?" Georgette glanced up, her face lit with a smile. "When did we start finding our social prestige was more important than our friendship?"

"I don't know." Catherine sank onto her chair. She should offer coffee or tea but didn't possess the energy to rise and ring the bell. "Perhaps when we started listening to others tell us what was expected of us."

"Marry well. If not money, then rank and family." Georgette perched on another chair, still holding the picture. "We don't have money like some of you have, but my mother's side has family back to the Mayflower. But you VanDorns have the income and the name. It's always eaten my mother and grandmother up with envy. They were convinced you would steal everything from my chances."

"And I did." Catherine stretched her hand across the desk though couldn't reach Georgette. "I don't intend to expose your little deception for what it is until you are ready for the truth to come out. There is nothing between Lord Tristram and me."

Her own deception.

How right Tristram was—no honor in deceit.

Georgette returned the picture to the mantel. "Which is why the two of you were in here alone."

"Some business with my late husband's estate." That, at the least, was true. "It won't happen again." She made herself smile. "In the event you decide you may like a title after all."

"Not his." Georgette studied Catherine for a few moments in silence, then nodded as though agreeing with an inner conversation. "You know, if Pierce believes you have a fancy for Tristram, and my grandmother thinks I am taking him from you, she will find the score has been settled."

More deceptions.

Suddenly feeling as fatigued as she had earlier claimed to be, Catherine wanted to go to her room and remain until Tristram left for home and Georgette got her own way. But the only way to manage all that was to discover how the gems had vanished from the safe at Bisterne.

Only one way to make that work—help Tristram discover the truth. After the charity tea, she would go into the city and do some sleuthing herself. She had a charity ball to help plan that would be her excuse.

"I want you to be happy, Georgette." She spoke that with utter sincerity.

"And I you." Georgette bounced out of her chair, rounded the desk, and embraced Catherine. "Now, what with this tea do you need my assistance?"

"I have no idea of the best way to set up the ballroom. Having it here would have been easier, but with two hundred people coming, that's just not possible. Should I have the tea table at the door or near the stage?" Catherine prattled on about table placement, the sort of beverages that would be served, the finger sandwiches, the cookies and cakes.

Georgette had attended several charity teas in the years Catherine was gone. She recommended the serving table be near the door, not the stage, so no one would receive lemon when they wanted milk because the music drowned them out. They discussed the decorations Catherine had planned and made arrangements to work on them the following day. They moved on to a discussion of the first skating party of the year. They did not mention Tristram again.

∾

Despite intermittent snow preceding the day, the morning before the tea dawned bright and clear. Catherine took the automobile to the clubhouse to look into the decorations, ensuring that the flowers had arrived on the morning train. They had, and she supervised their placement in the center of tables at which the guests could sit rather than balance a plate in one hand and a cup in the other as they needed to do at too many gatherings she had celebrated as a debutante. At last satisfied with the arrangements, she went home to dress.

For the second time since returning home, she donned one of her gowns from Paris. It was white lace with a wide neckline filled in from shoulder points to high neck with sheer lace. She wore only pearl eardrops and pearl combs for her hair beneath a wide-brimmed hat of white straw trimmed with white roses. White wouldn't raise as many eyebrows as had the mauve, and it still was not first mourning. She wished she could tell the critics that mourning a man who had barely acknowledged her existence was hypocritical of her. They would likely only tell her that she had married him and so her husband deserved her respect.

She cringed from the guilt. She hadn't respected him. Once she knew how he intended to continue to behave as though he had no wife, she doled out an income for him with a parsimonious hand. New laws gave her power over much of that income.

Her title gave her power over much of the Tuxedo Club's female population, enough that both elder Selkirk ladies bought tickets to the tea and arrived for the first time in five years. Their arrival brought a hush over the room—a hush followed by excited chatter. Catherine served them herself. Aided by Georgette and Mrs. Daisy Baker, another friend from Mrs. Graham's Academy, she dispensed tea and hot chocolate and directed the guests to the tiered plates of cakes and sweets. Daisy and Georgette had other ladies to serve, so the Selkirks had no choice but to come to Catherine or hold back and make spectacles of themselves.

"I see you heeded my warning," old Mrs. Selkirk greeted her. "Been behaving yourself."

"Yes, ma'am. Lemon or milk?" Catherine poured, sent for fresh tea, and poured some more. Her arm growing weary, but her heart singing at how smoothly everything was going, she poured one more cup, then glanced up to hand it to the next person in line and looked straight into Tristram's jade-green eyes.

He managed to take the cup and bow without releasing her gaze. "May I call tomorrow, my lady? I'd like to retrieve those earrings."

"I don't know." Catherine flashed a glance to Georgette, busy serving Ambrose and Florian.

"Tomorrow," he said, then left before she could protest.

The majority of the ticket holders having arrived, Catherine abandoned the tea-serving table and circulated through the room. On the stage, Estelle, Ambrose, and Florian played Christmas carols, then one of Estelle's compositions, then more music for the approaching season.

Most of the ladies and a handful of gentlemen greeted Catherine with cordiality, with only a few left-handed compliments slipped in.

"Lovely dress. You look more like a bride than a widow."

"Hanging out for another title?"

Catherine ignored the remarks and continued the hostess duties Mama had performed for the past ten years, begun soon after Tuxedo Park was built. Mama presided over a table, chatting and laughing with her friends, pretty and content.

Catherine paused beside her and kissed her cheek. "Are you happy with everything?"

"How can I not be when I have two such admirable daughters? And you and Georgette are friends again."

"That we are."

A lightness to Catherine's heart, she glanced around the ballroom for a glimpse of Georgette. She stood in the doorway speaking to someone out of Catherine's line of vision. The way she leaned toward the other person hinted at intimacy, a private exchange. A twinge in her middle sent Catherine's glance skittering around the room again.

Tristram sat at the next table with one other gentleman and three young ladies. Three more empty chairs suggested Estelle, Ambrose, and Florian had taken their refreshments there before going onto the stage.

Tristram and the other man rose at Catherine's approach. She didn't recognize him or the young ladies.

"Lady Bisterne," Tristram said, "allow me to introduce the Beaumonts. They bought the property next to the Selkirks' last year."

They all made proper "how do you do" responses, then the Beaumonts returned to their chairs.

Tristram turned to Catherine. "Catherine, you cannot continue to avoid me."

"In truth, my lord, I can." She motioned for one of the waiters to come clear away the dirty plates and cups left behind. "I hope you are enjoying yourself. And feel free to eat and drink your fill. We have an abundance of both." She glanced at Tristram's cup. "Hot chocolate? I thought I poured you tea."

"You did. It was not to my taste, and I was feeling rather chilled."

"But I ensured the tea was perfect. I don't know why—" She narrowed her eyes. "Are you all right? You've gone quite pale."

He was not only pale, a sheen of perspiration broke out on his face, and he gripped the back of his chair. "I think I should get some fresh air."

The brother and three sisters had ceased their conversation and were staring.

Catherine stepped forward to offer him her arm, but when he released the chair, he swayed, took a staggering step forward, and collapsed onto the ballroom floor.

CHAPTER 13

"Should a guest be taken ill, she must assure him that he is not giving the slightest trouble; at the same time nothing that can be done for his comfort must be overlooked." Emily Price Post

Catherine dove to catch Tristram before his head hit the floor. Around her, ladies gasped or emitted ladylike squeaks of horror. Before her, Mr. Beaumont reached Tristram first and lowered him the last few inches to the floor.

"Should I send someone to fetch the doctor, my lady?"

"Find a place to carry him first." Catherine kept her voice calm. To those who had seen the incident, she offered an assuring smile and waved hand. "He's a wounded war hero." She said the words as though that explained why he would collapse in the middle of her charity tea, while the music continued in joyous celebration upon the stage.

The explanation seemed to satisfy the ladies, for they turned back to their tea and cakes and chatter.

Catherine returned her attention to Tristram, so pale and motionless she wasn't entirely sure he still breathed. She wasn't entirely sure she still breathed. Her breath felt trapped in lungs about to burst with a wail.

"Please, Lord. Please let him get better from—something."

Tristram didn't drink spirits. He couldn't be inebriated. Unless he was truly ill or his concussion of two weeks ago caused some sort of relapse, he was ill for other reasons, something contagious.

No matter; she could catch the plague and she wouldn't care. She must see to his welfare.

"I live across the way in the bachelor's quarters," Mr. Beaumont was saying. "I'm happy to carry him to my room."

"Thank you." Except she couldn't see him there.

No matter on that either. Tristram needed warmth, comfort, and care. And she carried more responsibilities for this party that raised over a thousand dollars for buying gifts for less-fortunate children.

"Yes, carry him there. Thank you." As though nothing were truly wrong, she continued her circuit of the room, ending up back at the serving table, where Georgette seized her arm.

"Tristram? What happened?"

"He seems to have fainted. Dr. Rushmore is on his way, or should be shortly. Right now he's being taken to the bachelor house."

Catherine expected Georgette to say something about someone fetching the Selkirk car and driving him back to their house. Instead, relief smoothed her brow, and she nodded. "That is a good place for him. It's close. Shall we return to our duties at the tea table?"

Catherine agreed simply because she wanted to taste the tea Tristram had said was no good. She had assured herself it would be perfect, and when she tipped some into a cup, she found it delicious, quite strong enough for Tristram's taste. Perhaps he was already feeling unwell. The onset of influenza could make one's sense of taste go off.

Influenza was a frightening thought. People died of the disease. It was contagious, and this was a crowded room. If Tristram succumbed . . .

No, she would not think that way. The doctor was excellent. He would see Tristram to health again.

Worrying nonetheless, she dispensed a few more cups to some late-comers, including her brother and father. The latter took his cup and headed straight for his wife, but Paul Three lingered at the table—to talk to Georgette.

Catherine stared from one bright face to another, and the light dawned. Of course. Georgette and Paul had known one another all their lives. But did Paul truly want to break away from his well-ordered life? And why not? His elder and younger sisters did. Their poor parents, so sure they had done everything right, indulging their children perhaps too much. Yet the strictures of their society weighed heavily upon Estelle, with her talent that should not be wasted; Catherine, who had taken the sort of husband she had been brought up to revere; and now Paul, stuck in an office or on a train day after day for the next forty years or so.

As she supervised the clearing up of the ballroom, ordering the flowers from the table decorations to be sent to the hospital for the sick or the homes of a few people who were unwell or simply too infirm to go outdoors, Catherine began to think of ways she could help these two stop hiding their caring for another without having to wait until Paul came into his trust fund in two years. She simply had to get Tristram out of the way so the Selkirk ladies would not want a match there. Yet Catherine could not take him away from Georgette in their eyes. That would make matters worse.

The only solution was to find who had in truth stolen the jewels. Everything came back to that, to giving Tristram reason to go home.

Catherine could think of nothing to enlighten the situation further. Someone else had to have seen the jewels after her—seen them and taken them. It could only have been Edwin, yet when would he have had the opportunity?

Head whirling, she felt like Tristram had looked in those last moments before he fell—pale and shaken. She touched her handkerchief to her brow.

"Are you taken ill as well?" Georgette whispered in her ear. "I surely hope nothing was wrong with any of the food."

"I haven't partaken of any of the food."

But Tristram had. She had seen his empty plate dotted with bread crumbs pushed toward the center of the table, but she had not noticed a discarded cup of tea, now that she thought about it. The food came from a separate buffet table, but Catherine had dispensed the tea.

Her stomach seized up at the notion bouncing around her skull. Yet it wasn't out of the question. Someone, after all, lured him to Lake House, smashed him on the head, and left him in the snow. Hitting was more a thing for a man to do. Poison was considered a lady's trick. The blow had taken place outside her house, the illness at her charity tea— an illness that could have been caused by a foreign substance dropped into his tea. Two incidents easily blamed on her.

"Excuse me." Spinning on her heel, Catherine started to run from the ball room, realized that would draw too much attention to herself, and forced her legs to move at a sedate pace as though she merely left on some trivial business.

She couldn't race out of the clubhouse, either. Too many people, mostly the men dragged to the tea, filled the great hall or spilled onto the verandah despite the cold to smoke pipes or cigars. And the bachelor house across from the clubhouse was out of bounds to a female.

Not until she stood irresolute near the doorway did she think she should have attempted to retrieve Tristram's teacup. But no, she had ordered the waiters to clear the tables, an action that later could be taken as her trying to destroy evidence.

Her heart commenced racing like a polo pony. She pressed a hand to her chest and breathed deeply of a blast of cold air from the open door. It worked for a few moments until Dr. Rushmore strode through the doorway.

"Doctor?" She nearly pounced upon the poor man.

He touched her cheek. "You're pale, my lady. Are you ill as well?"

"Only anxious."

"He will do with a day or two of rest. Something he ate disagreed with him."

A new apprehension grabbed Catherine. "Do you think something could be wrong with the food? Will others be ill?"

And the charity tea a disaster.

Dr. Rushmore smiled. "I don't think so. Sometimes people can't tolerate certain foods. We don't know why yet, but we're working on finding out." He patted her arm as though he were old enough to be her father, which was decades from the truth. "I expect your beau will call as soon as he's well."

"He's not my—"

Several ladies emerged from the ballroom to surround the doctor, inviting him to come in for a hot drink and sandwiches. No one expected the doctor making a pittance in comparison with the income of the Tuxedo Park residents to pay for a ticket.

Like an automaton, Catherine returned to her duties. Guests were beginning to leave, drifting out in twos and threes, then greater crowds. She thanked as many as she could for coming.

At last, she was able to go home, where she buried herself in details for the next charity event, this one in the city, and tried not to think about Tristram. She could do nothing more than send a note around to Mr. Beaumont and request information as to Tristram's welfare. She received no response from Mr. Beaumont, nor from Florian and Ambrose. Instead, Tristram himself called on her the following morning.

∞

She received him in the conservatory, where sunlight shimmered off a row of icicles and the frozen lake beyond as though she resided in some kind of ice palace. The white snow and colorless ice emphasized the deep blue of Catherine's gown, and the sunlight brought out the red lights in her hair. The sight of her robbed him of breath.

"Are you going to come in or stand there and stare?" The corners of her lips twitched up.

He strode into the room to meet her in front of the windows where he had kissed her in a moment of madness he would like to repeat. "I was appreciating the scenery—and you." He shoved his hands into his pockets to keep himself from touching her. "Are you well?"

"I'm quite well. It's you who concerns me." She touched his arm as she gazed up at him. "Are you doing all right? Does the doctor know you're up and about? May I send for tea?"

He shuddered. "I think I'm off tea for a while, but I would like some of that hot chocolate."

She sent for the hot drink, then seated herself on a sofa to give him leave to be seated.

He took a chair adjacent to her so he could better look at her face, look into her eyes.

She met his gaze without flinching. "Were you poisoned?"

"We don't beat around any bushes, do we?" That was as much levity as he could manage, and he responded with his own question. "Why do you ask something so . . . serious?"

"Rarely does an illness come on so quickly, and you said the tea wasn't to your taste, but I made certain that tea was perfect. I put nothing in it but a little milk as you like it, so it should have been to your taste."

"Yet somehow, someone managed to insert a rather hefty dose of potassium bromide."

She jerked upright. "How do you know? The waiters cleared the table."

"Not fast enough. I regained consciousness soon enough to tell Beaumont to gather my cup from the table and give it to the physician."

"So you suspected, too?" She leaned back against the cushions and closed her eyes. "Did you suspect me again?"

"You had the best opportunity."

She opened her eyes wide enough to glare at him.

He leaned forward and covered her hand where it rested on the arm of the sofa. "Too good an opportunity. Like that last pair of earrings, it's too coincidental—too much like someone wanting me to think it's you trying to hurt me or get rid of stolen jewels."

"Hurt you?" She turned over her hand and laced her fingers with his. "Tristram, can potassium bromide not kill?"

"In large enough a dose, yes. Fortunately, that large a dose tastes so bitter, no one in his right mind would drink it."

"So whoever put it in your tea is an amateur at hurting—" She broke off, squeezed his fingers hard enough to hurt. "Let us stop dancing around this topic. Someone might have wanted to kill you. First the blow to your head in the snow, and now this."

"I have a feeling if you hadn't come along, someone else would have rescued me from the snow before it was too late. And today, again, I drank enough to make me lose consciousness for a few minutes, but not enough to kill me."

"So what's the purpose?"

"To scare me off from here? To scare me off from pursuing the jewel thief?" He rubbed his thumb over the back of her hand. "To cast more aspersions on you?"

"Or all of those choices."

"Or all of those choices."

"Who?"

The arrival of the hot chocolate saved him from having to hedge. He could tell her what he should have known all along, but he wouldn't again question anyone's honesty, as he had Catherine's, until he gathered enough evidence. But he needed her for that evidence.

"Tell me again, Catherine, what happened in those last days of Bisterne's life?"

She shook her head. "Nothing unusual. He came home for more money, as he did every quarter. He did some riding and shooting with a few neighbors, then he went to the safe, took out the jewels, and grumbled about how it was such a waste he couldn't sell them and not have to live off the largess of an American female. In short, it was nothing out of the ordinary."

"But why couldn't he sell the jewels? They go with the estate, but they're not entailed like property."

"I don't know. I thought some English law prevented him from doing so. Other than the combs and the wedding and engagement rings he gave me, I never wore the jewels. And the combs—" She stopped and her eyes widened. "He knew most of them were at least partially false. That's why he couldn't sell them."

Tristram inclined his head. "I think you're right. He knew all along someone had traded most of the real stones for false ones, but he might not have been sure which ones, so dared not risk anyone learning they were artificial if he chose the wrong ones."

"Someone else from the family. It had to be someone else from the family to potentially know the combination to the safe. His father, perhaps."

"Or his uncle?"

"Florian's brother?"

She did not suggest Florian himself, but with music drifting up from below, she must be wondering as much as Tristram was if Florian could be behind the attacks and the theft. It would explain his confidence that Estelle and her father would find him acceptable; he knew he possessed money hidden away somewhere, like a bank on the Continent.

"Was Ambrose ever at Bisterne?" he needed to ask.

She shook her head. "He despises the country. We met in town once or twice when I managed to get up there for some shopping. Why do you ask? He's not part of the family, is he?"

"No, he's a Wolfe with no Baston-Ward connections. But I'm seeking all avenues."

Her face lit, and she rested wide, sparkling dark eyes upon him. "Does that mean I am no longer guilty?"

"All the evidence tells me you are, but you, the person you are, says you cannot be." He drew her hand up and brushed his lips across her knuckles. "I want to call on you, but I need to find my answers soon. His lordship, my father, is getting restless."

"Why?" Catherine pressed the back of his hand against her cheek, then released him. "I understand that you are related through your mother, and I know my late husband's father was your father's friend, but why does this matter so much to him that he is willing to spend this much money to catch a thief?"

Tristram looked away, face growing hot. "To make me prove I am worth more than a failed soldier."

"How dare he hurt the lives of others just to make you prove something that's really none of your concern." With a swish of skirts, Catherine began to pace around the room. "This should be managed by a Pinkerton or whatever the English equivalent is. Scotland Yard is part of the government, is it not? Why aren't they onto the jewel thief?"

"To keep it out of public notice."

"Well, if you don't succeed, the public will notice eventually."

"I will succeed." He smashed his hand down on the cowlick, remnant of the injury he sustained in South Africa and right above the one he suffered on that snowy night almost below where he stood. "I have to succeed, Catherine. This has gone well beyond me finding a jewel thief. This pursuit could cost me my life."

"You are right in that." Her shoulders slumped, and her lower lip quivered. "We will think of something, I promise. In the meantime, please be careful." She stood before him, her eyes and parted lips giving him hope.

Footfalls on the steps warned him not to kiss her, but he would again, as soon as he could. Another reason to clear up the muddle with the jewels—Catherine.

"Be careful," she whispered before Estelle emerged to invite them for an evening of music.

Tristram was invited to too many activities for more than the briefest of moments with Catherine. At soirées and dinner parties, Georgette seemed to cling to him more than ever. During the day, Pierce kept Tristram occupied with excursions into the nearby forests for hunting, the results of which they either had cooked up by someone's resident chef or sent into the village to feed the poor. Tristram had grown up hunting and enjoyed the towering old trees around him, if not the taking of an animal's life so much. But the practice of chopping holes in the now solid ice on the lakes for fishing he could not comprehend. Why anyone would voluntarily freeze for fish one could well afford to purchase, Tristram didn't know, but Pierce and his cronies seemed to consider it a feat of manly virtue to withstand the cold for what amounted to only enough fish for hors d'oeuvres at a small gathering had they kept them.

Whether he was with a group of men or at a soirée, Tristram watched his back. He had escaped serious harm so far. A third attack might be the end. And if it was not, he would be leaving for England three days before Christmas to ensure he got home by the new year to please his father.

Not that going home empty-handed would please the marquess. He demanded full measure or nothing at all. In this, full measure meant the jewel thief and the rest of the jewels. For what purpose? So his father could be proud of him. And why did Tristram want that parental approval? In leaving the army, he showed that he didn't need it, so this time, his father tacked on the consequences to others, to people who desperately needed work and assistance. Without that, Tristram would forget the quest, send back the jewels he had found, and go about his business.

"I tell you, Tris," Ambrose reminded him for at least the twentieth time, "marry Georgette and all your problems will be solved."

Florian winked across the breakfast table where the three of them were still alone. "All except the little matter of him being in love with someone else."

"The woman tries to do you in, and you think you're in love with her?" Ambrose looked appalled. "Those blows to the head addled your wits."

"Even if she did try to do me in, which she did not, it doesn't matter. She won't see me as long as Georgette gives the appearance of dangling after me."

"Dangle is right." Florian grimaced. "She clings to you like a limpet to a rock. But as long as she insists on going everywhere you do, why don't you start going everywhere she does?"

"And encourage her?" Tristram glanced toward the doorway. Light, quick steps sounded in the hallway outside the dining room, warning that Georgette would be entering at any moment.

"Come to the VanDorns' with us this morning. Estelle has a new composition she wants to play for us."

Georgette entered, all so very pretty in a pink wool suit and creamy lace. She met his gaze and smiled, her eyes soft and warm. "You don't want to hear one of Estelle's compositions, do you,

Tristram? It's such a pretty day, I thought we could try the toboggan run at the racket club."

Florian cast him a sympathetic glance, then turned to Georgette. "Come listen to Estelle's composition, and then we'll all go over to the racket club. The ice is thick enough for skating."

"If you like, I'll go." Tristram didn't want to seem too eager.

For nearly two weeks after the December 2 tea party, he had enjoyed no more than brief moments in Catherine's company. Much of the time, Catherine was in the city working on charitable events and shopping with her mother and sister, Tristram learned from Florian. He moped around without Estelle near.

Tristram envied the younger man. If he were a free man, he could walk away from his father's edict, and offer for Catherine. Yet if he did, she might think he had chosen her as the easy road to income when his father withdrew his financial support.

The easy road.

Riding in the Selkirk automobile along the well-groomed street leading past houses that offered nothing less than ultimate comfort, Tristram realized that he had lived his life like that road. He had taken the path into the army because it was easier than fighting with his father about another course of action. He had disobeyed orders because that was easier than trying to convince his superiors that what they were doing hurt England's cause. And after, he accepted his father's ultimatum because it was easier than staying home. Believing Catherine was the jewel thief was easier than trying to find the real culprit. Now letting Georgette maintain her charade was easier than telling her she needed to be up-front and honest with her mother and grandmother and let him go.

No wonder Catherine would not fight for him when he was never fighting for himself.

He turned to Pierce, who was driving. "Let me down. I want to walk."

"We'll be there in two minutes." Pierce pointed out the obvious, but pulled on the brake.

"And I'll see you in ten."

"But Tristram," Georgette called from the rumble seat, "walking through this snow is so difficult."

"I know." Tristram waved and set off.

Belching and chugging, the auto pulled away, Georgette waving.

By the time he arrived at Lake House, his boots were sodden, his pant legs soaked to the knee. But his mind felt clear, and his soul unburdened. He had made his decision.

At the door, the VanDorn butler greeted him with considerably more courtesy than he had the last time and led him straight to the drawing room fire. And there sat Catherine dispensing hot chocolate. She glanced up, saw him approaching her, and dropped a china cup onto the hearth. It shattered into a hundred pieces, and Tristram's heart sang.

"I didn't know you were coming." She started to crouch down to gather up the broken china.

"Allow me." He stooped to gather the fine porcelain.

She knelt beside him. "Has anything new come to light?"

"Nothing." He leaned toward her, close enough to inhale her springtime fragrance. "I have missed you."

"You will have to miss me further when you return to England."

He rocked back on his heels. "What if I stay here?"

"If you inherit Cothbridge, will your people not need you there?"

"But I would rather—" He broke off and sighed. "Staying here is too easy, and I have just been castigating myself over always taking the easy route." He grinned. "Except for you. Nothing about you is easy for me."

She laughed at that, but before she could respond, Georgette emerged from the music room. "There you are, Tris. We are getting up a skating party. If we gather a few more participants, we can have races with the skating chairs."

"Skating chairs?" Tristram glanced from Georgette to Catherine. Both ladies laughed.

"The most absurd contraption on the ice," Catherine said. "I'll be happy to show—" She cast Georgette a quick glance.

Georgette's mouth turned down, but Estelle slipped past her with a trilling, "Excuse me. I am going to call some friends to get them interested."

One phone call by Estelle ensured that the racket club teemed with young people by the time the Selkirk and VanDorn parties arrived. Ladies and gentlemen alike donned black skates and headed to the lake. Someone found Tristram a pair that fit, and he donned them with considerable doubt.

"I haven't been on the ice since I was a schoolboy. We don't get weather cold enough to freeze a lake most of the time."

"It seems all I remember is freezing cold weather." Catherine shivered. "Living in Bisterne was like having an icehouse for a home."

"And not something you wish to repeat?" Georgette bent to strap on her own skates. "Last one on the ice is a rotten egg." She headed toward the ice.

"No takers, Georgie. We can't compete with you." Catherine glanced at Tristram without looking at him directly. "She has always been the fastest. That's why we let her push the skating chairs instead of riding in one like the rest of us ladies do."

"And where are these famed chairs?"

"On the lake." Georgette set out across the snowy ground as though walking in skates were as easy as walking in flat shoes. Catherine followed not as fast, but just as graceful as Georgette. Tristram moved more slowly, testing his balance on the skates. He hadn't been on blades for at least twelve years, and the iron runners didn't afford a body much support for someone unaccustomed to the sport. He wouldn't even think about how he'd fare on slippery ice.

Georgette reached the edge of the lake, stepped onto the frozen surface, and glided off like a swan, turning slowly, then spinning and leaping, creating a ballet on ice.

"She's beautiful," Catherine said.

"She is. Now, where are the chairs you were going to show me?" Tristram glanced around and saw two objects that resembled dining room chairs with arms and, on the bottom, runners attached from front legs to back on either side.

"What do you do with a contraption like that?" Tristram headed for the chairs.

"We'll show you." Estelle pointed toward one of the two lines forming. "You and Catherine go to that one. They need another female."

"They do not," Catherine said. "They have you."

"I'm going to Georgie's team." Estelle headed off at a trot. "I want to win."

"So do I." Florian sailed off after her.

"I think," Ambrose drawled, "those two are up to something."

Catherine shrugged. "As long as they are here in our sight, it can't be too bad. Will you partner me, Ambrose?"

"No, thank you." He scanned the line and headed for a pretty girl as yet without a partner.

"I believe," Tristram said, "we have been paired off."

"And Georgette doesn't seem to mind."

Unlike the other couples, Georgette stood behind a skating chair in which her male partner sat laughing.

Catherine's eyes widened. "Paul?"

Tristram took her arm. "Shall we join our team?"

They took their places in the relay line, and the game was on. The first two pairs arranged themselves at the edge of a marker made with someone's muffler. One of the men counted down to go, and the skaters shot out across the ice. They looked rather absurd, with the ladies' skirts flowing back along the wooden legs, and the chairs themselves sailing across the ice like bath chairs on a boardwalk. Most of the observers leaped up and down, cheering on their teammates. They laughed when one couple in the second run got skates, chair legs, and a torn flounce on the lady's gown tangled, and the two of them ended up sitting in the chair together. Whoops and hollers and cries to hurry rang through the crystal-bright air. The other team moved a full length ahead. Ambrose, surprisingly swift, helped make up some of the slack with his lightweight companion, also graceful and swift on her skates.

And then Tristram and Catherine's turn came.

Catherine settled into the chair and Tristram took his place behind, glad of the machine's support. He glanced at Georgette. Poised on her toes in the event her team needed her to go again, she grinned and waved them on. He smiled and returned his attention to Catherine. "Ready?"

"I'm ready." Catherine gripped the arms. "It's the return journey that worries me. I haven't skated in five years."

"It's been longer for me."

But they were off, too slow at first to please their teammates, then gathering speed as Tristram gained some confidence. They moved faster and faster, the cries of their team roaring behind them. Only a yard or two behind the other team, they reached the second muffler line marker. Catherine tried to stand. Her right foot shot out ahead of her. She grabbed the chair arm for support. With the rasp of steel on ice, the chair shot backward, knocking Tristram to the ice on one side and tossing Catherine to her knees on the other.

For a moment, neither of them made a sound, while their team shouted and groaned on the shore. Then Tristram grabbed the push bar for balance. Upright, he released the chair to go to Catherine's aid, and the chair soared across the ice, executed a pirouette, and came to a standstill a dozen yards away.

"The chair is a better skater than either of us." Laughing, Tristram reached down to take Catherine's hands.

She looked at him, eyes dancing as she struggled to get her feet beneath her. "We had better catch up with it."

"Then allow me." He tucked his hands beneath her elbows and lifted.

With the sun beating down, the surface had grown more slick. Both sets of blades took on minds of their own, and Tristram ended up on his knees holding Catherine far too close.

Or just close enough—close enough that the merest lowering of his head brought his lips in contact with hers.

From far away came a smattering of applause and a few hoots. For far too few moments, Tristram held Catherine to him, her lips warming beneath his. Then cold from the wet ice seeped through his trousers, and he remembered where he was and the size and makeup of the audience.

He raised his head. Her eyes were still closed, her face bright with sunshine and wonder.

"They're coming to our aid." He stole another quick touch of lips on lips. "Or perhaps to string me up."

"If they do not, your father will."

"I am done with being my father's pawn. If he wants to find the jewel thief, he can find him himself. I need to live my own life." He grinned. "Perhaps I will get a job."

"But all those people depending on the estate . . ."

"We can hope my father is bluffing. I don't know. I just know . . ." He trailed off.

Ambrose, Pierce, and Georgette sailed across the ice, their faces displaying amusement on Georgette and Ambrose's behalf, and confusion on Pierce's.

"I will not apologize." Tristram took Catherine's hand.

She shook her head and kept a grip on his fingers. His heart soared like the skaters racing toward them. She hadn't rejected him. She wasn't rejecting him.

Yet she still might if the faces of the others were indications of trouble.

Catherine reached out for Georgette. "I am so sorry. I never meant—"

"Never mind that." Pierce hauled her to her runners. "Your mother sent an urgent message for you to come home at once."

CHAPTER 14

"The bride gives a 'wedding present' or a 'wedding' ring or both to the groom, if she especially wants to. (Not necessary nor even customary.)"
Emily Price Post

Reality slammed into Catherine like a streetcar. What was she thinking, kissing Tristram—kissing Tristram in front of everyone. She was creating another scandal.

"What urgent message?" Catherine thought to ask as Pierce gripped her hand, pulling her toward the shore like a child's toy on wheels.

"I don't know. A call came into the racket club saying for you to go home immediately."

A crisis with one of the charity events, no doubt, a frantic hostess on the phone or sending telegrams.

Catherine increased her stride once on shore. "Where's Estelle?"

"I don't know." Pierce glanced around. "Expect she heard of the summons and left already. Get your skates off. I'll drive you."

Catherine complied, fumble-fingered and unbalanced in her haste. She looked around for Tristram. She saw neither him nor Georgette nor Paul. They didn't join her and Pierce in the automobile. Nor were they on the ice where a few people skated in a parody of a cotillion to the scratchy strains of an orchestra on a phonograph. Inside the Selkirks' automobile, Pierce was silent until he pulled the vehicle in front of Lake House.

"I suggest you go into the city for a few days." Pierce made no move to get out of the vehicle to open Catherine's door. "You've proven once again you can't be loyal to a friend."

"It's not like that. Georgette—" But she could not break a friend's confidence. That would be disloyal. Better to let Pierce and others think history had repeated itself until Georgette was ready to speak the truth to her family.

But history would not repeat itself. Catherine would not let herself succumb to the charm of another English aristocrat, probably one needing money as much as had Edwin, the Earl of Bisterne.

Except this was different. She loved Tristram. And if he loved her . . .

She might never be certain under the circumstances.

"Talk to your sister, Pierce." She tried to calm the roiling waters, then descended from the auto.

At the house, the butler flung open the front door.

"Lady Bisterne, so glad you're here. Mrs. VanDorn is in her boudoir."

Catherine raced up the steps to Mama's boudoir and opened the door without knocking. "Mama, what's wrong? Did Mrs. Rutherford fail to—"

"No." Mama slumped over her escritoire, a handkerchief pressed to her eyes. "Not that charity ball." She lowered the handkerchief and gazed at Catherine. "It's Estelle. She's eloped."

"But I just saw her . . ." Catherine sank onto the chaise longue. "No more than . . ."

When had she seen her last? Right before the races started. Thirty minutes? Forty?

"How do you know?" Catherine demanded.

Mama held out a crumpled and damp sheet of paper covered with musical notes on one side and scrawled writing on the other. Catherine took it and read the message in a glance.

Florian and I eloped.

"Not another one." Catherine dropped her head into her hands. "We can't bear another scandal. Estelle's reputation. Our reputation. Our family honor."

She had done damage to her family five years ago. She wouldn't do it again under any circumstances.

She squeezed her skull between her palms. "Did you tell Papa? Did you include Paul Three in the message from the racket club?"

"I haven't said anything to your father. Not over the telephone or even a telegram. Paul Three was no longer at the racket club. I have no idea where he went, so I'll have to wait until they get home unless you go into the city on the next train and tell them in person."

Catherine's head shot up. "It can wait until they reach home. There's nothing we can do from the city."

"You can make discreet enquiries about train passengers from here and in which direction they departed." Mama groaned. "Where have we gone wrong with our girls? It isn't as though we forced you into loveless marriages."

Catherine rested her hand on Mama's shoulder. "You were possibly too indulgent in allowing Estelle to devote herself to her music. Though not doing so would be a shame. She is so very gifted. And as for me . . . I let the hunger for status among the people here rule my heart."

But not again, not now with Estelle acting the fool.

She embraced Mama, then strode to the door. "I'll do what I can to find her."

She caught up a hat and her handbag from her room. "I may not return tonight," she told Sapphire. "I'll purchase what I need if it's not in the New York house." And then she ran down the steps, calling for the automobile to be brought around.

It already waited for her in the front, Mama having thought to order it. Catherine climbed in, and they chugged toward the gates and outside the fence to the train station, where another train wasn't due for an hour. An hour to wait, to pace around the waiting area, to fret over Estelle's madcap behavior, over her own folly in falling in love with Tristram, over her inability to set the past behind after all.

Seeing the stationmaster, she rushed across the room and plucked at his sleeve to gain his attention. He had known her family for years through their dozens of journeys along the forty miles to the city and back. He had been the last familiar face in Tuxedo Park who had seen her when she eloped. "Sir, can you tell me what train Miss Estelle VanDorn took?"

"Miss Estelle?" He scratched his head beneath his railroad cap. "Hmm. I don't believe I've seen her today."

Catherine stepped back as though shoved. "Not on a train? Then how——?" She clamped her mouth shut. "Thank you."

If she hadn't taken a train, how had they departed? They wouldn't have access to an automobile. But Florian could drive a carriage.

She left the station and headed through the village to the livery. Her actions were going to create a stir. They wouldn't be able to keep Estelle's elopement with Florian quiet for long. That didn't matter if Catherine could bring Estelle back. Once she returned, any hint of gossip would die down. People would put the temporary disappearance down to a youthful lark.

When Catherine hastened into the livery, the liveryman was just unharnessing a horse from a buggy, the former looking weary. He shouted something to a stable hand, then approached Catherine, his face puzzled. People from inside the fence rarely rented horses or buggies from him.

"Ma'am?"

"Has a young man rented a horse from you today? Dark hair, green eyes, about this tall?" She held her hand a few inches over her head.

The liveryman nodded toward the horse the hand led toward the stable. "That one. Reserved him two days ago and picked him up around two hours ago. Just sent him back lathered like he'd been in a race. And if he takes sick 'cause of it—"

"Send the bill to the VanDorn household. Where did he come back from?"

"The man didn't say. Just left him here and walked off." He narrowed his eyes. "Is there something illegal at foot?"

"I don't think so. Just a guest being foolish." She offered him a winning smile and retraced her steps to the train station.

The man would have to get back to wherever he came from somehow. If he didn't have a vehicle, the train was the only way.

The train she intended to take into the city had departed, and a lone passenger slumped on a bench. Catherine approached him, too conscious of the stationmaster staring at her from behind the ticket counter. "Did you just deliver a buggy to the livery?"

"Yes, ma'am." The man didn't bother to rise. "Got paid well for it, too, and to keep quiet about where."

"How well?"

He told her. She paid him twice as much to talk. And then she sat to wait for the next train. Outside, dusk fell. Incoming trains began to disgorge passengers returning from the city, businessmen from New York. She scanned the crowds for her father, then thought to duck her head so none of the others who knew her would see she sat waiting for a train alone, a train that arrived at last, delayed by snow upstate. Down the line everything remained clear, giving Florian and Estelle too much of a head start.

Catherine sprang to her feet and headed for the doors, pushing against the inflowing tide of city workers.

"Catherine?" Her name rang out over the general hubbub of greetings, continuing conversations, and a few tearful departures. "Catherine, wait."

Catherine spun around on the edge of the platform. Surely her ears deceived her.

They did not. Georgette shoved through the crowd and grasped Catherine's hand. "Thank the Lord I found you. Your mother said you probably left already, but I had to try. I'd have come after you—" She stopped to catch her breath. "You must come."

"Come where?" Catherine blinked in confusion.

"All aboard," the conductor bellowed.

"I have to get on this train," Catherine said.

"No, you have to come back to my house." Georgette dashed a hand across her eyes. "It's Tristram. He—"

The train's whistle blew, drowning her words.

"He's been badly injured." Georgette's shout cut through the whistle, the hiss of steam from the boiler. "He's asking for you."

The train would leave in no more than a minute or two. Catherine must be on it or Estelle would be lost somewhere in the myriad choices of trains pulling out of Grand Central Station or lost somewhere in the city, even a ship across the Atlantic.

"I have to be on that train." Her heart constricted.

"He could die if his injuries are bad enough." Georgette grasped Catherine's shoulders and shook her. "If you don't come, then you truly have betrayed our friendship because you don't deserve a man who loves you as he does."

"My sister . . . The scandal . . . I—"

"Last chance, ma'am," the conductor called to Catherine across the empty platform.

Perhaps her last chance to see Tristram, her last chance for love. She could lose him forever. Estelle was lost only in the meantime. Estelle had made her own choice to create a scandal. Mama had made the choice to keep it quiet and not send out wires that could have stopped her younger daughter.

If Tristram was injured, it wasn't by choice. If Catherine chose not to go after him to protect her family's reputation, it was her choice and the sort of selfish action that had caused so much trouble in the past. If she wanted to truly set the past behind her, she needed to go to Tristram and show him that she put him first.

She waved the conductor on and turned to Georgette. "What happened?"

The train doors closed, the whistle blasted again, and the train drew forward, gathering speed with every yard.

Georgette tucked her arm through Catherine's and dragged her toward the exit. "He was walking down the hill to see you at Lake House when the brake on an auto failed and struck him down."

"An auto." Catherine pictured the heavy machine barreling down the hill, striking him, crushing him. "Who . . . whose auto was it?"

Georgette sighed with a catch in the middle of the exhalation. "Ours."

∞

Tristram raised his lids to see Catherine gazing down at him with eyes as soft as velvet and her hand holding his. He managed a smile. "I needed to see you."

"I wasn't here." Her fingers tightened on his. "I was trying to catch up with Florian and Estelle. And not—" A hot tear splashing onto his hand. "I was so concerned about preventing another scandal, I wasn't thinking of you at all, while you—" She gulped. "I've been so concerned about appearances and other people's unforgiving natures, I've forgotten what's most important—loving others."

"You're here now. That's what matters." He closed his eyes again, aching all over from what he understood was a few bruised and broken ribs, a sprained wrist and ankle, and more bruises. About the only part of him spared by the speeding automobile was his head, spared when he dove headfirst into a snowbank as he tried to escape the runaway vehicle.

One more attempt on his life, this one coming too close to success to be brushed aside for the sake of not making his father angry. The someone had to know he had left the Selkirks' and headed down the hill.

He knew the answer. Of course he did. But Dr. Rushmore had made him drink what felt like a gallon of chloral hydrate for the pain, and his brain felt too fogged to think.

"I'm here." Catherine drew his hand to her cheek, then rested it on the coverlet again. "So are Georgette and Ambrose and Pierce."

"Florian? Where?" Tristram levered himself up on one elbow. "Where is Florian?"

"Later." She smoothed hair back from his brow with a cool, gentle hand. "When you're more awake."

"Where is Florian?" He would ask the question until she answered.

"May as well tell him," Pierce's voice rumbled across the room.

She sighed. "Florian seems to have eloped with my sister."

"Did he?" Tristram started to chuckle. A stab of pain sliced through his ribs, and he stopped the mirth. "He'd better marry her, or I'll take drastic measures."

"He'll marry her." Ambrose sounded disgruntled. "Some men enjoy charmed lives. Florian gets his heiress. You get yours. Me, I get nothing."

"Heiress." Tristram tried to pull his thoughts together. "The young lady in New York?"

Ambrose snorted. "Nothing doing there. No title and no money equals no heiress."

"I have little enough to offer a bride." Tristram managed to open his eyes wide enough to look into Catherine's. "Perhaps a true title in a few years, but no money."

"You could still find the thief by your father's deadline." Her smile was probably meant to be encouraging.

He shook his head, making it swim, but held his ground. "I've given up on that. I can't risk my life nor that of the lady I love just to impress him."

"It is past time you admitted that," Georgette spoke across the room.

"But, Georgie—"

"Quiet, Pierce. I have never been interested in Tris."

"But who—?"

"Me," Paul Three said from the doorway.

The resulting exclamations made Tristram's head ache.

"Go away, all of you." Catherine moved away from the bedside. "He needs rest."

Sleep was what the doctor had recommended for him, and his limbs felt too heavy, his mind too slow for speech. His eyelids drifted shut. He fought the impulse. He needed to say something important, ask something important. A runaway car. A driver masked behind goggles and muffler and hat. Something . . . Something familiar . . .

Sleep took over his will, and he woke to the sound of muffled voices.

"If his sister-in-law has a boy, you'll have nothing but a useless courtesy title." Ambrose spoke with a sneer to his voice. "His father is going to cut him off, Tris has been such an embarrassment. He has no standing in society. They all know he was asked to leave the military, even if we pretend he resigned on his own."

"Do you think that all matters to me? I had a title once. I haven't seen it's brought me anything but misery."

"And you think he loves you, not your trust fund? Ha." Ambrose's bark of laughter held no mirth.

Tristram stirred, wishing for the strength to shout Ambrose down about such a notion.

Catherine's hand tightened on his, almost as though warning him to remain quiet. "If that is the only way to have him in my life, he may have my inheritance."

"Love and money." Ambrose sounded more sad than bitter now. "Some men get everything, and some of us nothing."

"Perhaps you need to find work for yourself," Catherine said, "even if it's not right for an English gentleman. It's not that way here."

"I don't know how to work unless I join Estelle and Florian making music. And for what? Coins tossed to them on the street? But then, Estelle has enough money not to stoop to that sort of life."

"If my parents allow her to have it."

"They will, and Florian won't mind about the jewels any more, but his brother and my uncle will never give up on getting back what's theirs." Ambrose began to pace, his heels clunking on the wooden boards, then silent on the rug, and back again to the boards. "I'm only good at gaming."

"That's it." Tristram mouthed.

Catherine smoothed her fingers over his. "And spending it or losing it again. You must have won a fortune from my husband. Did he not pay you?"

"Oh, he paid me—in false coin. That is to say—" Ambrose didn't say what he intended. He collapsed onto a chair.

And the drug washed from Tristram's brain as though a tidal wave had swept it clear. He rose on his elbow and grasped Catherine's wrist. "False . . . coin." Each word hurt to speak. "False coin."

Her eyes wide, she stared back at him. "As in false jewels."

"No, no, I didn't," Ambrose cried. "I couldn't. The jewelry was in the safe."

"No, it wasn't, was it?" Catherine rose and walked to stand with her back to the door.

"Don't," Tristram gasped out. "He's dangerous. He tried to kill me."

"I did not. You're family. You're my friend." Ambrose shook so badly Tristram saw it from across the room. "I wouldn't have let you die. With the snow, I was angry because my heiress rejected me for a German baron three times her age. And the tea? I just wanted to scare you off hunting the jewels or think it was Catherine or . . . I didn't try to kill you. You weren't truly dangerous to me."

"I am one more barrier to the title and potentially an heiress," Tristram said between shallow breaths.

"That auto nearly killed him." Catherine's tone was as hard as real diamonds.

"It got away from me. I thought he'd get out of the way in time." Ambrose's pitch rose like someone on the edge of hysteria or an act of violence. "I've sat vigil here for twelve hours because I was afraid. I'm not a murderer."

"No, just greedy." Tristram's eyes burned. His heart ached with pain worse than his broken ribs. "If you weren't family, I'd have worked it out sooner. But we've been friends all our lives. You didn't shun me when I came back from Africa. Or so I thought." Spent, he sank back onto his pillows, a lump rising in his throat. "Suspected Catherine. Suspected Florian . . . Believe me, Ambrose, if I legally could, I'd give you the title. I don't want it."

"Well, you have it." A hard edge rang through Ambrose's words. "A telegram came yesterday morning while you were cavorting on the ice. Her ladyship, the viscountess, has safely delivered a girl, albeit early."

Tristram's heart sank. "I'm sorry. I don't want it."

"No, but you get it. You get everything. And I—" Ambrose sprang to his feet. His chair crashed to the floor as he sprang toward Tristram.

"Run," he managed to gasp out before Ambrose pressed a pillow over his face.

He clawed at his cousin's hand. He may as well have tried to move a boulder with a teaspoon. The pillow remained, blocking off breath, sending spots dancing before his eyes and blood roaring in his ears.

A scream and another crash penetrated the waterfall blackness. And the pillow sailed away. Air rushed into his lungs so fast his ribs protested.

"Tristram." Catherine rested her hands on either side of his face. "Look at me."

He looked at her. He smiled.

"Thank you." She was breathing hard and weeping, but smiling. "I, um, hit him over the head."

"How fitting. Better ring for help."

But the door burst open, and Mrs. VanDorn, Paul, Georgette, Pierce, and three footmen burst into the room. Confusion reigned for several minutes, and in the end, the footmen carried Ambrose away, and Pierce volunteered to call the police. Through it all, Catherine stood beside Tristram, holding his hand until quiet settled over them.

"You can't stay alone with him in here," Mrs. VanDorn said. "Not more than a minute or two alone." She left, allowing the door to hang open an inch or two.

Tristram turned to Catherine as far as he could move and gazed into her lovely eyes. "I'm sorry, Catherine. I know it's not what you want, but I do love you. Can you marry me and live in England with a future marquess?"

"As long as I'm married to you, I love you enough to live with you under any name in any country."

EPILOGUE

"A wedding in very best taste for a widow would be a ceremony in a small church or chapel, a few flowers or palms in the chancel the only decoration, and two to four ushers. There are no ribboned-off seats, as only very intimate friends are asked. The bride wears an afternoon street dress and hat. Her dress for a church ceremony should be more conventional than if she were married at home, where she could wear a semi-evening gown and substitute a headdress for a hat. She could even wear a veil if it is colored and does not suggest the bridal white one." Emily Price Post

For once, Estelle did not insist on providing the music. Carrying a bouquet of yellow roses and wearing an indigo gown and wide-brimmed hat trimmed in indigo ribbons, she stepped out of the music room and headed up the aisle made by the rows of chairs set up in the VanDorn drawing room. Forty friends and family members turned to watch her, some with disapproving frowns, some with raised eyebrows, most smiling.

No smile could be as wide as Catherine's. Not even Estelle's heart could sing as loudly as her elder sister's as she clutched her father's arm from inside the music room and watched her beautiful, talented sister glide up the room toward the fireplace, where her new husband stood as best man to Catherine's groom.

"Even if she did elope," Catherine murmured to Papa, "you should be proud of her."

"We are." He cleared his throat. "Even if they went all the way to Virginia to get married. If she'd waited a bit, we might have given our permission."

"It's the 'might have' that was the difficulty." Catherine patted his arm. "They'll make you proud."

"As traveling musicians?" He shook his head. "Outrageous."

It was rather, but Catherine had never seen two people so happy—unless it was Tristram and her.

Three things brought them moments of sadness, though, which was more bittersweet than regretful—the surprise that Georgette was not there to be Catherine's attendant. With the VanDorns' blessing and a lecture on not being honest with his parents, Paul had taken her sailing for Rio de Janeiro the previous week. They intended to explore the Amazon, the farthest life from Tuxedo Park she could imagine. Far from seeking freedom, Ambrose waited to learn whether he would stand trial in America or England, as he had committed crimes in both countries.

The biggest source of Tristram's flashes of regret was that he hadn't heard a word from his father since telegraphing the news regarding Ambrose six weeks earlier. Catherine hoped that the marquess would at least acknowledge their wedding.

But Catherine brushed those gloomy thoughts behind as a quartet played the wedding music behind her, signaling her moment had come to walk toward her groom. She wanted to run.

The minute she stepped through the drawing room doorway, she felt his eyes upon her. Along the length of the chamber, she met his dark green gaze and held it. The closer she drew to him, the more she read tenderness, love, and approval. She hoped he liked her gold satin gown and wide-brimmed hat with filmy gold veiling floating from the brim. She certainly approved of his black suit, white shirt, and inability to tame his cowlick. The errant curl made her smile. He returned the smile, and the guests sighed.

She reached Tristram's side and handed Estelle her bouquet of creamy roses. Papa set her hand in Tristram's and stepped back to make room for the pastor.

"Dearly beloved, we are gathered here—"

The drawing room door flew open. "So sorry to interrupt."

Everyone turned toward the newcomer, a tall, elegant man in late middle age with light brown hair going gray and familiar features.

Catherine caught her breath and looked up at Tristram. Barely healed from his injuries, he had grown pale and swayed forward half a step.

She slipped her arm around his waist. "Are you all right?"

He shook his head. "Father, what are you doing here?"

"You did send me an invitation." The Marquess of Cothbridge strode up the aisle and gripped Tristram's shoulder. "I tried to get here sooner, but it's difficult getting across the North Atlantic this time of year. You couldn't have waited until spring to get married?" He glanced at Catherine and bowed. "But of course not. How do you do, my lady."

Catherine opened her mouth, but no words emerged.

"Better if I sit down and let this ceremony continue?"

"Yes, my lord."

His brows arched nearly to his hairline at her forthright response, but he merely inclined his head and accepted the seat a footman provided.

"Continue." Tristram directed the pastor in a voice that quivered with what some might have thought anger, others distress, and Catherine knew from the faintest twitch at the corner of his mouth to be suppressed laughter.

His face bemused, the pastor continued with the ceremony. Tristram and Catherine spoke their vows and, against custom, exchanged rings. Then, with Tristram's hand covering Catherine's where it rested on his forearm, they recessed to the drawing room door to greet the well-wishers.

While the guests filed into the dining room for the wedding tea, the marquess held back so that he was the last to approach them. He bowed, then gripped both their hands. "I, um, owe you both apologies." He cleared his throat.

They gazed back at him.

"For what, sir?" Tristram asked.

"For being ashamed of you. For sending you into danger. For not listening when you tried to tell me about your work with the former soldiers. When I learned you were nearly killed—" He scowled. "From others, not you, I must note—I realized I'd, uh, been so determined to have a son who did the things I thought would make me proud that I didn't realize I had a son who had already done things to make me proud." He kissed Catherine's cheek. "I like your wife. She spoke her vows like your mother did—like she means every word."

"I do." Catherine smiled, her heart swelling with joy.

Tristram slipped his arm around her shoulders. "And I love her rather intensely, the more for the fact she has put my accusing her of theft and worse behind us."

"Then I have hope that you can put everything I've said and done to you behind you," the marquess said.

Still holding Catherine, Tristram reached his free hand out to his father. "I already have."